I0742862

Blame it on the Pumpkin

Horror Tales for Halloween

Edited by Tara Moeller

ISBN: 978-1-954214-15-6 (OpenDyslexic)
978-1-954214-16-3 (Déjà vu)
978-1-954214-17-0 (ePub)
978-1-954214-18-7 (Kindle)

CONTENTS

A Note about the Cover

The cover art was created by Brit Austin Art and turned into our lovely cover by Portfoli-Mo.

Read more about these artists—and find out where to see more of their art—on the back pages of this book.

FROM PUMPKIN TO JACK-O'-LANTERN

Nonfiction
By Marjory E. Leposky

How does a pumpkin turn into a jack-o'-lantern? It all starts in the spring after the last frost, when the ground is warm – but don't plant them too early. Otherwise, they may ripen and rot before Halloween.

Growing pumpkins begins with plowing the ground. First the growers plow the ground. If they planted a cover crop in the fall to protect and enrich the soil, they turn it over in the spring before planting.

Two different ways exist to plant pumpkins on a large commercial farm. Both involve a tractor that pulls a drilling machine. In direct seeding, people sit on the drilling machine. At regular intervals, they drop seeds into holes drilled into the soil to a specific depth. Transplanting involves growing seeds in a protected place and then dropping the young seedlings into the prepared holes.

Either way, the layout of the field depends on whether the crop will be irrigated; whether it will be weeded by hand, with a plow, or with chemicals; the height of the mature plant; proper sun direction and coverage; the soil type; whether the rows will be covered in plastic; and how any fertilizer might be applied. All of this is carefully planned before any planting takes place.

In a small plot or back yard garden, a person might use a hoe or shovel to make the holes about four feet apart.

Typically, two seeds are planted in each hole to improve the odds that at least one will grow. As the plants sprout and develop leaves, growers typically remove the weaker ones, giving the stronger ones a better chance to grow and produce fruit.

Pumpkin blooms need bees for pollination, so the growers always have beehives in their pumpkin fields.

Vines come up, and pumpkins grow on the vines. The pumpkins sit on the ground, unless the growers spread straw on the fields to prevent them from rotting.

In September, the growers harvest by hand. They walk through the fields and find ripe, damage-free pumpkins with the correct shape. They cut the stems one day, allow them to dry, and pick them up the next day.

The workers line up these pumpkins along the drive rows (the paths in the fields where the tractor will travel). Then they drive through the fields with the tractor, pulling a flat-bed trailer full of large cardboard bins. (They don't harvest pumpkins in rainy weather because the rain causes the bins to get wet and fall apart.)

They pick the best pumpkins, with the best stems. Some may weigh 25 pounds or more. Workers on the ground toss pumpkins up to workers on the trailer, who fill the bins with 40 or more pumpkins per bin.

Once the bins are full, the workers take the pumpkins to the grower's warehouse. The same day or the next, other workers driving forklifts load the bins into tractor-trailers to go to wholesalers, who distribute them by truck to individual retail stores.

When the pumpkins arrive at the grocery store, they are unloaded and arranged at the front of the store to attract customers.

To choose the right pumpkin, look for one with a flat surface without bumps so you can cut into it. Very carefully load the pumpkin into the car. Wrap a seatbelt around it like a small child to transport it home. Bring the pumpkin into the house and put it at the center of the dining room table to await the arrival of Halloween.

Carve the pumpkin on Halloween Day. Clean off the dining room table and lay down newspaper. Set out a large bowl, a large metal spoon, and a large cutting knife.

Before you start cutting, decide what you will do with the pumpkin after Halloween. If you plan to eat it, or to recycle it at a wildlife center that will feed it to raccoons and opossums, don't draw on it with a pen, pencil, marker, or anything else. Free-cut it – and be careful. You don't get a redo.

First, cut inward at an angle around the top of the pumpkin, holding onto the stem. Then pull the stem and the top upward to make the lid. Using the spoon, scoop the pumpkin flesh and seeds into the bowl. Then dig into the pumpkin to remove all of flesh and seeds.

Now inspect the pumpkin and decide where to cut into its body to make the eyes, nose, and mouth. Cut inward at an angle, and put the pieces you've removed into the bowl.

Now you have your jack-o'-lantern. As the sun goes down, use a non-drip wax candle that you can reuse the next year. The wax is not good for the raccoons and opossums.

An average-sized pumpkin contains a cup of seeds. Pumpkin seeds can be eaten, dried or roasted. Many people like them – and so do birds and squirrels.

The first Halloween I carved my own jack-o'-lantern, we had a second full moon of the month – a relatively uncommon event called a "blue" moon.

The next day we carefully loaded the jack-o'-lantern into the car with a seatbelt again. At the wildlife center, our jack-o'-lantern joined a table full of others waiting to be animal food.

Blame it on the Pumpkin

MOONLIT HUNT

Flash fiction
By J. M. Silverleaf

Silvery waves shimmer on the night breeze.

A silhouette appears on the rocky shore,

splayed claws that rip and rend, long snout

upturned toward the bright full moon.

The branch creaks beneath my weight,

heightening my fear, pine-scented.

A snort. The head turns.

Cold fear trickles down my spine.

Run!

Blame it on the Pumpkin

PUMPKIN HOLLOW

By Pamela Kinney

Rotting jack-o-lanterns and dead corn stalks appeared in a field overgrown with weeds. A silent, tall figure parted the middle of the stalks and stepped out. It was a scarecrow. It held a large black and orange envelope with writing slashed on it and a stamp with a jack-o-lantern in one gloved hand. The scarecrow tossed it into the air, and a sudden tornado of wind snatched the envelope and swooshed it away. The heavy, lingering scent of pumpkin spice, chocolate, and dying autumn leaves remained, but within seconds, that too disappeared like a specter. The scarecrow and the field faded, leaving behind only mocking laughter filling the air.

After doing her usual 2-mile run, Penny made a stop to pick up her mail before heading indoors into her apartment. One envelope caught her eye. It wasn't because the envelope was black and orange, though that did stand out among the plain white ones, most of those being bills. Or that it was bigger than the rest. No, she thought she detected a scent from it, mixing with the cool late October air; dying autumn leaves, pumpkin spice, and chocolate candy. Then it was gone, like a distant memory.

She unlocked the door to her apartment and stepped inside, hitting the light switch to light up the living room. She dumped the mail on the coffee table, shrugged off her jacket, and tossed her keys onto the couch. The mysterious piece of mail held her interest more than rubbing her aching feet or taking a shower.

She slit the envelope open with a fingernail and withdrew a single orange card with black words. Each letter raised from the cardstock, reminding her of shiny black oil.

"Come out to Pumpkin Hollow, Virginia on All Hallows Eve to enjoy a Halloween festival and a special haunt in a cornfield on the edge of town. It all begins at five o'clock and ends at midnight. See you October 31st."

Penny frowned. *I never heard of Pumpkin Hollow, and I've lived in Virginia all my life.*

The card had directions to the town, with GPS coordinates too. It appeared to be in Nelson County, a couple of hours away. No website link or phone number to call for information.

Really? In this day and age, for any company or town to not have a website or even a phone number for any questions?

Penny enjoyed Halloween and loved being scared visiting the haunts that popped up everywhere beginning in September. But she had no wish to drive to a town she never heard of even for some Halloween celebration. There were places closer to home here in Richmond. She didn't toss it in the trash. Unable to let go of the card, she sat down on the couch and stared at it in her hand.

Something about it. Something called her. Just something....

She took her cell phone from her purse and tapped a phone number. Her friend, Chris Thompson, picked up.

His sleepy male voice drawled from the other end. "What's up, Penny?"

She smiled. He always had that ability to do make her feel good. Penny had been friends with the charming oaf since middle school. They both worked at Capitol One.

"You want to check out a new haunt on Halloween, Chris?"

"I thought we got them all and agreed on doing King's Dominion's Halloween Haunt?"

Penny picked up the card, staring at it. "That was before I got this invitation in the mail for a Halloween celebration that includes a special haunt in Pumpkin Hollow."

"Where? Pumpkin what?"

"A town called Pumpkin Hollow. It will have a Halloween festival and haunt. The directions came with the invitation. The town is about two hours away, in Nelson County. I never heard of it either, not until today."

"Must be a one-horse town if neither of us heard of it. The haunt probably is a bunch of local kids from the town's only church who will dress up in Party City costume rejects and hide in some cornfield maze."

The card slipped from her hand to land back on the pile of mail on the coffee table. The card's earlier scent reappeared, stronger this time, and wafted to her nose. Determination rose in her breast.

"Chris, I'm doing it. I'm going to call Lynda and Judi and see if they will do it too. Are you in or out?" Perhaps that odor meant to seduce her to want to go; it succeeded. Elation filled her with a fever pitch.

"Well...."

"Look," she said, exasperated, "if nothing else, we can leave early enough to stop for lunch somewhere and maybe if there's enough time, we can stop at some farm or farmer's market to pick apples. The leaves will have all turned and the colors will be gorgeous. I know it may not even be in the same class as King's Dominion, but I got this crazy feeling it will be a night that we won't forget. I don't know why, but I do."

"All right. I'm in. Can I bring my new girlfriend, Annie?"

"Sure."

"Well, gotta go, so I can call her. And Penny."

"Yes?"

"I'll drive us there in my SUV, your car is tiny."

"Thanks."

He hung up. She made two calls, one right away to Judi Manitoc, the other, thirty minutes later to Lynda Thompson who wouldn't get home until then. When Penny had gotten ahold of both women, they agreed to go. Of course, they would. Like Chris, she knew them since middle school,

they, her, and Chris, all Halloween fanatics. A town none of them never heard of, its name sounding very Samhain, with a haunt it would be holding on Halloween. It called to their little orange and black hearts.

Just as she headed to the kitchen to make her dinner, her cell rang. It was Annie Sanders, Chris's new girlfriend.

"Annie here."

"I know."

The other woman sounded puzzled. "Wait. How did you…"

"Caller ID."

"Oh, yeah, I'd forgotten about that. Anyhow, calling to tell you, I am going. Chris knows I am not into that scary gore stuff, but…he is cute." She giggled. "Gotta go. See you Halloween morning."

Once the call ended, Penny noticed that her phone needed charging. Once it had been plugged in, she made it to the kitchen this time without interruption.

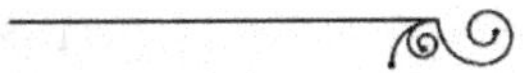

Her head hit her pillow, and once Penny fell into the realm of Nod, she dreamed. She found herself in a field of pumpkins. Not pumpkins, as all had faces carved in their orange flesh. Grinning faces, evil sneers, laughing ones, every kind of expression she could imagine. Penny stopped over to pick up one small, white jack-o-lantern. It looked like it asleep when suddenly, it popped its eyes open. She yelped, almost dropping the little squash.

"Hey, Penny, we're waiting for you. We've been waiting for you, and your friends, for a long, long time. Five of us would like to leave this cursed land."

Shaken, she dropped the pumpkin. It hit the ground with a hard thud. It managed to roll over to reveal a smashed-in face with one eye melding with the other one, its mouth molding at one end to give it a nasty sneer.

"Do you think this is only a nightmare?" said the jack-o-lantern. "Well, guess what? It's not! We can't wait for you to get here."

A stream of black shadow rose from the pumpkin's openings, high and higher until it was the same height as her face. Her heart jerked, and her palmed sweated as she saw two red eyes in the middle of the darkness before it rose higher into the sky, cruel laughter erupting from it.

Penny sat up with a shriek. Her heart sledgehammered against her chest, and her nightgown, sheet, and blanket had glued to her sweaty body. She couldn't remember the nightmare, but fear from it still held her in its grip. Still shaking, she tumbled out of bed and ran to the bathroom, where she kneeled before the toilet and threw up. Finally, her stomach emptied, and with the shakes gone, she sat there for a while before she got off the linoleum to tear off her wet clothing and toss it in the dirty clothes hamper. After a shower, she made it back to bed, where she drifted off, but this time nothing haunted her dreams.

The next morning, Halloween began cool and crisp. Nestled in her jacket, Penny only took her wallet, house key; a few more needed things she'd tucked in the pockets of her cargo jeans. A few minutes later, a black SUV rolled to a stop alongside the curb. Chris was driving, Annie sat in the passenger seat beside him. Lynda and Judi huddled in the backseat. They all tumbled out of the vehicle as Penny stretched, tested her door one last time to make sure it was truly locked, and jogged over to join them.

"Ready to go?" asked Chris with a grin.

"Definitely."

"Well, get in," said Judi, "I didn't have breakfast and I'm hungry."

Lynda gave her a look of affection. "You're always hungry, even if you've already eaten."

"Yeah, well, it's true, I'm starving."

Everyone popped inside the vehicle and Chris started the engine. He guided the vehicle into the street but jammed on the brakes, locking the tires, just as a speeding car streaked at them. At the last minute, it swung around them and roared down the street, an orange blur.

Chris cussed. "What the hell?"

Penny pressed a hand over her thrashing heart and with her other shaking hand, death-gripped the top of Annie's seat in front of her. "God, that's close. They almost hit us." A quick glance showed her all the others' white faces. "We would have been hurt, or worse."

A nervous laugh came from Chris. "Maybe this is a warning that we shouldn't go to Pumpkin Hollow."

Lynda's color returned to her face. "Really? This is not a horror movie. We made plans for this Halloween festival and haunt in this boondock town I never heard of, so let's get going. Wish I'd gotten that jerk's license plate number though; I would dial the police."

Penny sucked in air as her heart returned to its normal pace, and brought her hands back to lie on her lap. She noticed the others looking better.

Chris glanced back at her and nodded. "Are we still going?"

"Yes, we are! Lynda's right. It's Halloween, but things like that happen all the time, every day. Nothing weird about that."

Judi, who sat in the middle between her and Lynda, mumbled. "I hope you're right, Penny. Kinda odd. That car was painted orange. Like a pumpkin."

Penny turned to stare out the window, but she didn't see the flash of passing scenery as Chris drove his vehicle down the street.

No, nothing weird at all. The person just owned a car painted orange or maybe Lynda thought it colored orange. It might have been brown or some other color.

Except you saw an orange car, too.

She turned back to Judi. "That's just a coincidence. I think we all have Halloween on the brain."

Judi nodded. "I guess you're right."

"I know I am."

Chris found a fast food place, and he went through the drive-thru and ordered them all breakfast. He parked his SUV so they could eat the food, tossing the trash in a trashcan nearby before he started the engine, and left the parking lot for the street.

Judi took her black sweater decorated with sequined, dancing skeletons off her lap and drew it up to her chin, shivering. "Is anyone else feeling nippy? Chris, can you turn up the heat?"

Chris replied, "The heat is on. If I turn it up anymore, we'll all roast."

Judi didn't say anything else, just huddled in her seat. Penny would have agreed with her about it getting colder in the car, except no one else complained. The chill reminded her exactly what those ghost hunters on TV said about spirits when they were in a room. After a while, the iciness left, and she curled into the window and watched with drowsy eyes as Chris merged his vehicle with others on 288. In another fifteen to twenty minutes they would be on Route 60 and heading west. She fell asleep.

Penny found herself in a daydream. She stood in a field full of pumpkins and started walking. Nothing scary, nothing weird, only pumpkins, some orange, others were white as a ghost. Ahead, she saw towering mountains.

Blue Ridge mountains? Although, she'd never been to them as she didn't do hiking or care to muck around much in the country. Except for haunts and corn mazes—she did go to various country farms that did those.

Suddenly, she almost ran into a deer. Funny, considering a wild animal like a deer would have taken off at a human this close. But again, this was a dream. There must be different rules for a deer in a dream. Right?

The animal had big, brown eyes and stood about the same height as her. She didn't see any horn or nubs for ones on top of its head, so she guessed it must be a female. They called female deer does, didn't they? The closest she ever got to a deer would be in a zoo or at

Maymont Park or roadkill from one hit by a vehicle.

"Taking your time getting to Pumpkin Hollow, aren't you?" said the doe. "We're waiting for you."

Penny awoke with a start, and when her pounding heart settled to a regular steady beat, she straightened in her seat, trying to get the kinks out of her neck and shoulders.

That had been a strange dream—nothing scary about it, except that a deer talked to her. Still, even though her heart drummed normally, she felt an unsettling disquiet. She forced herself to look out the window and focused on the scenery.

The sun shimmered in the blue sky. The leaves on all of the trees on both sides of the highway were a kaleidoscope of browns, oranges, reds, and autumn golds—an endless parade of costumes ready to be judged. Penny loved this time of year. Maybe it symbolized death to come with the imminent arrival of winter, but to her, it meant just another aspect of the goddess Hecate that those long, long ago, believed in. Autumn became the crone on the verge of dying. With spring, came rebirth.

Summer was the young woman. A never ending cycle.

Before she could ask where they were, she bowled into Judi as the SUV almost zigged off the road to the left. It missed tumbling into the ragweed-covered ditch before Chris fought with the steering wheel and won, zagging it back onto the road. Thank God for her seat belt. Her fingers touched cool glass and she saw a deer dart into woods on her side of the car. That unsettled her further due to her daydream.

She turned away from the window. "What happened? I saw a deer."

Chris answered. "Sorry. We almost hit the damn animal. It just stood in the middle of the road! I slammed on my brakes, but the SUV skidded to the left." He pulled the vehicle over to the right side and turned off the engine. "Is everyone all right?" He sounded unsteady.

Annie giggled, more tense than giddy. "We almost had roadkill."

Chris retorted, "Almost a wrecked truck, too." He spoke louder. "You know, for a sec, I swear, that deer's eyes glowed and its whole body faded. But it had to be my imagination. You know, Halloween on the brain; ha, ha." He joked, using Penny's favorite phrase.

Snoring filled the vehicle and Penny turned to find Lynda fast asleep.

Judi shrugged. "She's been like that ever since we passed Powhatan. Same for you, though you didn't snore." A snicker escaped her. "Some people can sleep like the dead through anything."

Chris restarted the engine and drove back onto the road.

Penny called out, "Hey, Chris, where are we?"

"We made it to Nelson County. Those GPS coordinates you gave me have taken us off 60 and onto this stretch of road. We've been on it for the past fifteen minutes before the kamikaze deer. Nothing to be seen but mountains and woods, and the occasional farm."

Penny stared through the windshield. Chris was right. Mountains loomed on each side of the road like sentinel giants. No other vehicle on the road. Just them. She assumed others had gotten the invitation in the mail like she had. Either they had already reached Pumpkin Hollow, or decided to get there around the time the festival began.

For a second, the woods surrounding them had grown...darker. Ominous. *Clouds*? She looked up at the sky. Nothing but sunshine and not one storm cloud in the sky. Mystified, she looked at the woods again, but everything appeared normal. She settled back in her seat.

They passed farms with fields full of drying corn stalks, apple trees full of the fruit, and pumpkins. Farm animals fed on long grass in some pastures. A small herd of dairy cows, another of Black Angus cattle, and horses. One meadow even held alpacas.

Chris said, "Down this road for a mile and by the GPS, we make a last turn onto a road called of all things, Last Road, and drive on it for a bit before we arrive at Pumpkin Hollow."

He made that last turn and Penny noticed rows of pine trees on each side of the road, bending over like drunken old men snatching at each other. It felt like they'd entered a dark tunnel made of the trees. The SUV rolled through it for a few minutes. When it ended, they found endless fields fertile with crops on both sides of the road.

No birds of any kind, not in the fields, or even up in the sky. No cows, horses, or other farm animals either. Just corn, apple trees, and pumpkins that stretch for acres and acres. Some of the pumpkins were almost as big as her mini coupe, while none seem to be smaller than a pony. Pumpkin Hollow must be doing well; other parts of Virginia had suffered a drought for the past couple of months. Funny thing, she'd never seen pumpkins as gigantic as these, except on TV.

Penny said, "You know, the pumpkins in the fields before we turned on Last Road were ordinary in size. These look like they should be in the Guinness book of records."

The corn bothered her. She knew by this time in Virginia, most of the corn had been picked and the stalks dying. These on the other hand, still looked green, with plenty of ears of corn.

Annie pressed her face to the passenger window. "Where are all the animals? No cows or horses at all." She sounded letdown.

Instead of disappointment, the lack of farm animals unsettled Penny. Why, she couldn't put a finger on it, it just did.

They drove past a large orange sign that welcomed them to Pumpkin Hollow in black letters. Pumpkins and corn stacks leaned against it.

Judi reached out to shake Lynda awake. "I swear growing up, my parents and I traveled all over the Commonwealth and I never knew this place existed."

Something in the distance caught Penny's eye. *What's that?* As they drew close enough, they saw the biggest scarecrow any of them had ever seen, in the middle of a corn maze at the edge of the small town. A sign hanging on an empty booth outside the gate proclaimed it to be "The Sacrificial Maze." *The haunt?* A tall man stood by the booth. He opened the gate and stepped into the field, vanishing among the cornstalks.

The town itself was quiet, with no sign of a festival or life even. Penny glanced at her watch, shaped like a ghost, and saw that it was two o'clock.

She said, "The event begins at five. Shouldn't there be people getting the festival ready? Where are all the vendor tents? The food trucks?"

Chris said, "I admit it looks odd that nothing is set up, but we're here and I don't know about you, but I'm hungry. Let's find somewhere in town where we can get something to eat."

The town had only a main street and a couple of other roads. They only saw a tiny grocery and a few other shops, all closed.

Lynda called out, "Hey, there's an eatery."

A lit sign above the door said, "Pumpkin Hollow Diner."

Chris parked alongside the curb right in front of the building. Penny and her friends got out and Chris locked the SUV. They walked up to the café's door and tested it. It swung open with ease. Muted lighting did not hide the fact no one sat in any of the booths or at the tables. The room looked forlorn. A young woman who looked to be in her early twenties stood behind the diner counter, dressed in a waitress uniform that could have come straight out of Mayberry. She looked washed out, her skin pale, with dull eyes and hair. As if someone had pushed a button, she straightened and became animated, rushing over to them.

"Here for lunch?"

"Not too late, is it?" asked Lynda.

"Oh no, we can still serve you lunch. There are five of you? How about this table over here?" She guided them over to a large, oblong table with a red and white checkered plastic tablecloth near the double doors that led to the kitchen.

Penny stared at the bright colors of the tablecloth. Minutes ago, the room and its furnishings appeared dingy. Just like their waitress. Maybe she needed food. Maybe a glass of wine would help, though she doubted this place had that on the menu.

They sat down. Judi and Lynda stuck their purses down at their feet beneath the table. Annie obviously had Chris to pay for anything. Penny fished her wallet from her cargo pants.

The others gave the waitress their orders, so when it came her turn, Penny picked up the menu the waitress handed her and made a quick decision, passing the menu back. "The burger combo, please. Medium-well. With a salad instead of the fries. Coffee with cream."

The waitress flashed her a smile. Fighting the need to bolt from the café, Penny gripped the edge of the table and shook her head. She thought she saw a vision of a predator's glistening, sharp canines.

Not real. Not real.

No one else appeared to have noticed. She looked up at the waitress again, and only saw a young woman's face with frown lines in her forehead.

"Can you bring me a glass of water, please."

The waitress nodded. "Sure." She hastened off.

Penny waited until the woman was out of earshot, leaned over the table and whispered. "I think maybe we should leave. There's something wrong with that waitress."

"Chris snickered. "What? I know that woman looked like she's on her last legs or something when we first walked in, but I think you just need food."

Penny hissed at him. "Keep your voice down. I don't know what's wrong, but I swear as soon as she smiled an image of a hungry, snarling wolf with fangs hit me. Look at this town. Where are the people?"

Annie picked at a cracked nail, but looked up when Penny finished. "This is a farming community. Maybe this town has people working their fields until close as possible to when the Halloween festival begins. It starts at five, right?"

Putting it like that, Annie made sense. Although, what about those from out of town? Penny felt pretty sure they must have mailed off invitations to others besides her. It bothered her about who even knew about her love for Halloween haunts, other than her friends.

She withdrew the orange envelope from an inside pocket of her jacket. Just as she had smelled at her mailbox, the odor of dying autumn leaves, pumpkin spice, and chocolate candy teased her nose.

Chris sniffed the air. "Hey, that smells like pumpkin pie. I bet they're baking it. I might order a slice of that for dessert." He licked his lips.

Annie shook her head. "Pumpkin pie? I smell chocolate candy. Like those little candy bars they hand out to trick-or-treaters. I love chocolate."

Penny couldn't believe it. "You guys caught the aroma from the envelope, too, didn't you?"

Judi flashed her a funny look. "That scent came off that envelope?"

"When I first took this envelope out of my mailbox, its scent was overpowering. Actually, three smells in one. Then the odor vanished. I thought it came from my mind. Until now."

"No doubt they sprayed some type of cologne on it," said Lynda. "To remind people of Halloween."

"A cologne that smells of three distinct odors in one?" said Chris with an underlying sneer. "Where would they get it? From the dollar store?"

Lynda shook her head. "It doesn't matter where they bought it. Or if they sprayed it. I've smelled scented envelopes before. Nothing out of the ordinary."

The envelope fell from Penny's fingers onto the table and she stumbled to her feet. "Hey, where's the waitress with my water? She's been gone ten minutes. Did she have to go draw it up from a well?"

Annie's chair screeched as she stood. "I'll go see why she's taking so long."

Chris reached out to stop her, but his fingers met empty air as she headed toward the doors that led to the kitchen. No noise came from behind them. No talking, banging of utensils, anything. Annie pushed one of the double doors open and stepped inside. Seconds later, her scream broke the silence.

"Annie!" Chris leaped up and his chair crashed on its side. He busted through the doors. Everyone else followed.

Annie stood plastered to the wall, her eyes bulging and her face bloodless. A low keening issued from her parted lips. Chris grabbed her and shook her.

"Annie, knock it off. What's wrong?"

Lynda let loose a long hiss. "My God." She lifted a trembling hand and aimed a finger like an arrow at something at the far side of the dim kitchen.

The waitress hung on the wall, her arms outstretched, slashes over her body, and black holes where her eyes had been. A wreath made of autumn leaves crowned her head. She had been crucified. The cook lay on a butcher's block with lettuce and spinach stuffed into his mouth. He looked like he was only sleeping, but they knew the truth. Jack-o-lanterns sat scattered around the kitchen. Every
one of them has a lit candle inside

"Where's the blood?" said Judi, her face pallid. "There should be blood everywhere."

The dread inside Penny grew colder. "How could anyone kill the waitress and the cook, arrange their bodies as they did, and bring in and light all those jack-o-lanterns? I doubt the cook had them in the kitchen."

"And who could manage to wipe up all the blood and we don't hear a peep? We didn't hear screams." said Lynda.

Annie ran to Chris, pressing herself to him and burying her face in the crook of his neck. She said, "I want to go home, Chris. I told you

I'm not into Halloween like you." Her sobbing grew louder. "Now look what we've gotten into. Two people murdered and we might be next."

Lynda nodded. "I hate to say it, but I agree with her. I'm dialing 911 to get whoever constitutes for the law in this town, report this, and hopefully we might get home before dawn." Her gaze shifted to the bodies. "If we're lucky."

She dug her phone out of her purse and before she even tapped the numbers, cursed. "My phone's dead; I know I had it fully charged before I left home. Anyone else?"

Penny and the others tried theirs, but they had the same results. Dead phones, or no signals.

Penny wrapped her arms around herself. The shudders started small, growing until she was surprised that she could move when everyone left the kitchen. This began feeling like one of those creepy Halloween slasher movies to her.

Chris headed for the door. "I'll try my phone outside. Maybe something in this place is keeping ours from working. Come on, Annie." His arm around her, the couple walked out the door.

"What the hell!"

Penny heard Chris loud and clear. Once she stepped out into the cool, crisp air, she understood. First, it was no longer daytime, but night. No stars, just a crescent moon. They'd arrived in town at two. There could be no way they had sat in that eatery for hours. Just as frightening, Chris's vehicle no longer sat at the curb. Or anywhere nearby as they walked first one way up the block, then down the other way.

Annie moaned. "This isn't funny, Chris. Where's your car? I want to go home."

Chris whipped around. The glare of the diner's sign bathed his face in red light, giving him a distorted mask of reddened flesh, as he had his lips in a snarl, and his eyes flashing.

"First, stupid, it's not a car, but an SUV, like a truck. Do you think I snuck out somehow and drove it away to hide it?" He shoved his face close to the frightened young woman. "You didn't want to go with me to try out this haunt. You should be glad I wanted to date you, whiny, self-serving idiot!" His spittle splashed her face.

Annie flinched and stepped back, only stopping when she backed into Judi. Judi put her arms around her and glared at Chris. Lynda joined her and did the same.

Penny said, "What's wrong with you, Chris?"

Chris spat at the sidewalk and took off, running down the street until they lost sight of him. What scared Penny more than the dead bodies in the diner, the sudden night, and Chris's vehicle missing—the unflappable Chris had turned into an abusive creep.

She turned to the other women. "This isn't like Chris. I've known him since middle school and he never spoke to anyone like that, especially women."

Lynda sniffed. "Well, he acted like a jerk just now."

They needed to find the law and report the victims in the diner. Then they would go search for Chris and hopefully, by that time, he settled down and had found his vehicle so they could all go home. When the police let them go, of course.

Someone, or more than one person, appeared to have taken Halloween to a whole new level. Whoever, whatever, they succeeded in scaring Penny. She grabbed her cell phone and tried 911 again. Still dead. The others had the same problem with theirs. Moving down the street didn't help.

"Our batteries died?" asked Penny. "Though for all for our phones' batteries to have died...."

Lynda's face tightened. "I'm betting this whole town is a dead zone. Maybe the whole area. The farmers around here must use landline phones."

Judi called out, excited. "Maybe that man with those two kids over there can point us to the police station. Or maybe his cell phone works."

A tall man and two children stood at the end of the sidewalk, the red light from the traffic signal flashing on them and giving them a bizarre, bloodied appearance. It didn't matter. They needed to report the crime, so Penny and her friends approached them.

Her fingers barely grazing the man's shoulder, Penny said, "Excuse me, sir, but do you have a working cell phone, or can you point us to the police station in this town?"

The man and the two children turned together at the same time. Penny backed away. They wore masks and Colonial clothing. The little girl had golden ringlets gathered on each side of a plastic mask with its mouth opened in a scream. Her dress was pale blue with white lace that almost met the top of her boots. She was missing her hands, though. The other child—a boy—wore ragged brown pants and a long, white shirt crusted with dirt. His feet were bare even though the night air held a chill to it. His mask had the face of a snarling bobcat's. The man, dressed in pantaloons and an opened, blue frock coat over a white shirt with a laced front, white stockings and buckled shoes, also he wore a mask with no mouth or nose. She didn't see any eye holes, but the mask might have slits. Being dark, she wouldn't have seen those.

They're dressed in costumes. Nothing scary. He must be taking the kids trick or treating, or to the festival. Penny drew closer to the man again.

Over Annie's whimpering, Lynda's whisper came to her ear. "Penny, come back. There is something's wrong here. Can't you feel it?"

Penny found herself close enough to be able to peer at the man's mask, to find the eyeholes. Her breath caught in her throat and she stumbled backwards.

No eyes! The mask had no eyes!

It's an illusion. Or my eyes playing tricks.

She got within a hair's breadth of him again and reached up, touched the mask. Ice cold. Not plastic, instead it felt like papier-mache. A sudden wind from out of nowhere snatched it from the man's face. It flew away into the night.

Oh God. That can't be real. She stared in horror at the man's face. Or the lack of it.

Oh God, oh God, oh God.

Screaming filled the air and she realized that it came from her. It rose in crescendo, as her friends' own screams joined hers when the three strangers metamorphosed into glowing orbs and dissipated.

She staggered back to her friends. "Did you see that?"

Judi's skin had lost its color. "They disappeared like…. ghosts."

"There are no such things as ghosts," said Lynda, but the undertone of her voice contradicted the words.

Penny's heart battered against her chest. "You saw it. I saw it. Judi saw it. Annie, you saw it too, didn't you?"

Annie didn't reply. Penny, Lynda, and Judi turned around to look. Annie was gone.

"Where did she go?" Judi said.

Lynda said, "She was just here with us."

Up the street from them, Annie's voice shouted. "Hey, I found Chris! He's—"

Her shrieks filled the night. Ignoring the blinking red traffic light that still hadn't changed to green, the women dashed across the street and down the next block. They never found her. The buildings stood silent and dark. They tested all the doors, but they found every one of them locked. None of the scared women felt foolish enough to venture down a pitch-black alley between two of the buildings. Annie never answered their calls either.

"First, we find people murdered, then Chris runs off to find his stolen car, and now Annie has gone on ahead and now has vanished after we hear her screaming. What is happening?" pleaded Judi. Her voice revealed how close she hovered to the breaking point.

"Please, calm down, Judi," said Lynda as she patted Judi's arm.

Judi snarled at her. "Calm down? Calm down! If it hasn't hit you yet, *there* is something wrong with this damn town. We've gone down the rabbit hole not to some crazy wonderland, but Hell. We're losing our people, one by one, besides Chris's SUV. I haven't seen any cars since we've arrived either. So, ditch the *everything is fine.*"

Lynda dropped her hand. "I admit, it looks bad. Where's the police station? I didn't see one back by the diner and every place on this block is closed."

Penny snapped her fingers. "Remember that field with the scarecrow at the edge of town? Let's head there. I saw a man by the booth when we first drove into town."

Judi cursed under her breath. "If we get out of this nightmare, I'm not doing haunts on Halloween again. The scariest thing I'll do is hand out candy to kids at my apartment."

Penny agreed. "We get out of this, and I'll buy the candy and help you hand it out."

The traffic light died at that moment. As if on cue, clouds passed over the only source of light they might have had, the crescent moon. Worse, none of their phones could be used as flashlights, so that really meant the batteries had died. Not able to see each other, they grabbed each other's hands and blundered through the dark.

Penny wished she'd thrown that card away. If she had, she and her friends would have just gotten through King's Dominion's Halloween Haunt and would be at some restaurant, enjoying good food and each other's company.

Ghosts. What about those three ghosts?

A chill rushed up her spine. "I hope we survive the night, otherwise, we might be ghosts haunting this place."

Lynda said, "What did you just say?"

Penny lied. "Nothing. Look! We must be near that field." She stopped and narrowed her eyes.

"I think that might be it, across the road."

Not seeing headlights coming from left or right, they crossed the road. Penny glanced back over her shoulder at the buildings. They seem to have merged with the night.

They found that not all lights had been extinguished. A floodlight attached to the fence shot a beam of light through an opening.

"Where's the booth?" said Penny. "It's gone, just as where the hole is now, there had been a gate."

One by one, they climbed through the opening in the fence and stepped onto a field littered with dead corn stalks. The flood light showed them the beginning of a path that led into the upright stalks.

Penny said, "The field had green corn stalks loaded with corn when we got to town earlier."

Judi inched closer. "More proof something is off with this town. Why don't we just go back to the main road and walk away from here?"

"Judi," said Penny, "We don't have flashlights to help us find our way. And remember, there are ditches on each side of the road. We might trip into one of those and break a leg." She took Judi's trembling hand. "If we wait until first light, then we can hike out of town."

"I agree with Penny." Lynda's voice coming from behind them made them jumpy. They turned and saw her. "Besides, someone killed that those people back at the diner and going down a darkened road, well, I don't want to meet the killer."

They used the path through the stalks. The glare from the floodlight only reaching so far, they grabbed each other's' hands when the dark enveloped them.

Judi broke contact when she walked off path into the stalks. She squealed and stopped. Penny and Lynda bumped her. "Maybe there's more than one killer. We only saw that waitress, the dead cook, those ghosts, and that man Penny saw in this field when we first came to town. If he's alive, where's he now? Everyone that lives here must be dead. Those ghosts, they might have been killed, the man's face sliced off by one of the killers."

"The little girl had no hands—they could have been hacked off for some sick reason," said Penny. "But again, she's a ghost. Maybe she couldn't materialize all the way. I saw that on TV once. That headless ghosts are not really headless, just not fully formed."

Lynda whimpered. "I don't care. I just want to go home."

They moved deeper into the stalks. What seemed hours, but no doubt had been minutes, Penny and Judi stepped from the stalks into a wide circle strewn with dried corncobs. Lynda was not with them.

Penny called out, "Lynda?

Nothing.

"Lynda?"

Still no reply.

Her voice echoed in the air. Realizing what she might bring upon their heads, she shut her mouth. *Dummy, just let the wrong people know where you're at.*

Judi shook Penny's shoulder. "Look, a green light. Something's inside it. Must be that scarecrow. Perhaps that man you saw is with it, and maybe Lynda too."

Worried about Lynda, Penny took Judi by the hand and they proceeded with care. They stepped into the green light. No sign of Lynda, though.

The light flooded the small area, but Penny couldn't see where it came from. A tall figure sat on a throne made of rotting pumpkins, corn, apples, and straw. An old-fashioned scythe lay across its lap. The stench of overpowering decay punched at Penny and Judi.

Judi flinched. "That godawful smell." She hunkered over and puked.

Penny's felt nauseous too, but she fought it. When she turned away, she saw three figures on the ground nearby. Her friends, Chris, Annie, and Lynda, all asleep on strewn corncobs.

She drew closer. Her breath caught in her throat. *No.*

Not asleep. Dead. Not a mark on them, but what looked like leaves from corn stalks covering the ground like a mat beneath them.

Their eyes popped open. Penny shrieked and stumbled back, tripping and landing on a pile of dried corncobs, rotting pumpkins and apples. The departed Lynda flashed Penny a knowing smile.

Lynda said, "Not murder. Sacrifice. This town makes sacrifices every year on this day. They lure fools to come here at Halloween. Over two centuries ago, on All Hallows Eve, the townspeople murdered what they thought were five witches in their midst. Instead, those witches were innocents. Because of that heinous crime, the townspeople cannot enter Heaven, but the Devil made a bargain with them."

The corpse continued. "They are stuck here every Halloween to repeat what they did to those people. Once five innocent souls are sacrificed before midnight, the town vanishes in limbo until the next Halloween. Five murderers get to enter Hell while the five just killed take their place to haunt this town the next Halloween. The faceless man is the town leader. The Devil stripped him of sight, smell, and taste for his wrongful judgement." The corpse's smile grew as wide. "They've got quite the racket here, don't they?" Lynda closed her eyes.

The figure rose from its macabre throne and Penny saw it was the man without a face. He stood, holding the scythe in his hand.

Penny scrambled to her feet. "Oh, God, Judi, run!"

Judi turned, but ran straight into the arms of two men dressed in Colonial garb who appeared out of nowhere. They dragged the screaming woman over to the faceless man. The faceless man swung the scythe high in the air. The instrument came down once, twice, and a third time. The two men dumped the dead Judi at Penny's feet. Penny screamed.

Penny was next. The fifth sacrifice.

Heart hammering, she bolted and pass through a mass of shifting shadows that filled the field. The dead townsfolk? Other sacrifices from the past? It didn't matter, for she saw an opportunity. A narrow opening, but she took the chance.

She sped through several spirits in front of it, glad for once that she ran every morning. Not looking back, tripping a few times, but always regaining her footing, she sprinted out of the field and onto the road that led out of the town. The angry roars of those she left behind told her she shouldn't stop. Couldn't stop. Focused on her escape and it being too dark, she slammed into the trunk of a tree. This time, she lost her footing and fell into a hole. Or a ditch. Her head hit the ground hard and she lost consciousness.

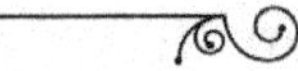

"Hey, she's waking up."

Penny opened her eyes and through the pain pounding in her head, she saw the faces hovering above her. She screamed and struggled to sit up, to get away. Fought the hands, trying to hold her down.

"Hey, hey, lady, we're just trying to help." The voice came from a man.

She blinked and saw the people that surrounded her, many dressed in costumes and makeup, others in orange T-shirts and jeans. The shirts had *Pumpkin Hollow Haunt* in black scrawled across the front. Behind them stood more people dressed in costumes and street clothing. Some of those worked at pushing aside others to get a better look.

"Pumpkin Hollow is a haunt?"

The man who'd spoken to her, moved to let a paramedic drop down beside her, while he replied, "Well, yeah. You paid a ticket to go through it." The man lifted her arm and she saw an orange paper bracelet wrapped around her wrist, *Pumpkin Hollow Haunt* scrawled in black text across it. "See this? It means you paid to walk through our attraction."

"Is this Nelson County?"

"Nelson County? No, you're in Goochland."

"My friends. Where are they?"

The man frowned. "Friends?" He called out. "Are her friends here?"

No one came forward. She allowed the paramedic's assistance to help her sit up and she searched the throng of bodies, but she didn't see a sign of her friends. Managing to get to her feet, she pushed the medic aside and dashed off before he could stop her. She shoved past crowds leaving the haunt, and darted inside, past costumed volunteers in Colonial clothing, bloodied and pale like ghosts.

"Hey, what are you doing?" yelled one of the haunt people. "You're going the wrong way, lady!" She ignored everyone as she backtracked though the haunt, trying to find Lynda, Judi, Chris, and Annie. Just as she arrived at the first room, hands gripped her shoulders from behind and yanked her back and almost off her feet. Frightened, she lashed out. Two hands imprisoned her arms by her sides and a face came into view. It was the haunt worker who'd spoken to her outside.

"You're freaking out those who paid to come in here. That is our haunters' jobs to do. Not some whacked-out woman."

The paramedic finally caught up, and he and the man led her outside and to the ambulance. Its revolving red light reminded her of the red traffic light in the cursed town. The paramedic led her to the back of the van as the haunt worker headed back to the haunt. The red light from the ambulance bathed the paramedic's face for a second, and she thought she saw the faceless man. When she got inside the vehicle, she saw his dark skin and that he had two eyes, a nose, and a mouth. Just an ordinary living man.

Another paramedic assisted him into strapping her onto a gurney before loading her into the back of the ambulance. The first paramedic got behind the driver's wheel, while the second one sat beside her.

That man smiled as he took her blood pressure. "We're taking you to the emergency room at Henrico Doctor's Hospital. My partner, Jim, says there probably nothing more wrong with you than a bump to the head, but it's better safe than to be sorry. They can do x-rays and a lot more than we can."

Once they arrived at the hospital, they rolled her inside. The nurse put her in a cubicle and left her alone while she went to find the doctor. Penny sat on the edge of the bed. Suddenly, the ceiling light in the cubicle died. Fighting the disquiet that arose in her, she slipped off the mattress to discover what happened.

She thought that maybe she should stick her head out and call for a nurse when the toe of her shoe hit something on the floor. It slid away. She picked it up and drew back enough of the curtain to let in light from outside to see what it was. Her heart pummeled her chest. A smashed pumpkin. The ceiling light came back.

A prickling sensation stood her hair on end. She sensed a presence behind her. Her hands grew clammy and with shaking limbs, she turned.

The scarecrow towered over her. Before she could scream for help, he swung his scythe, and she never felt any pain as the sharp point connected with her chest.

Before the scarecrow ripped her soul from her body, she heard a voice in her head. *No sacrifice ever escapes Pumpkin Hollow.*

Vampire Gourd

By Jennifer Kyrnin

"You must use old, unaltered blood," the gardening clerk called out. "The new stuff won't take, and you'll be stuck with a bucket full of bloody soil."

I ignored her and carried my bag of potting soil and the receipt for my vampire seeds to the front registers. Did she think this was my first growing season?

Normally I'd have my potting soil sent to me directly from Transylvania. Everyone said the soil didn't matter, but I had won the tri-county fair "Largest Blood-Sucking Plant" award three years in a row and I didn't like changing my methods. But when I'd gone to their site this February, the 404 message showed the site was down.

Blame it on the Pumpkin

I dug through my receipts from the previous year and found a phone number. The texts seemed to go through, but no one replied. In desperation, I tried phoning and got a computerized voice telling me that the number was no longer in service.

For a frantic number of days I searched, texted, and called anyone and everyone for a source on Transylvanian vampire dirt, but that market had dried up and I couldn't understand why. None of my European contacts would call me back, and Nigel, the Scottish gardener I'd worked with for three years, hung up on me when I asked him about it. It was like there was a giant conspiracy to hide something sinister.

For a moment or two, I considered flying to Transylvania myself and getting the dirt direct from the source. But the growing season was nearly here, and I had an order for seeds coming in to Molback's in the next twenty-four hours. And there was the cat. I couldn't leave Diamond alone, she'd probably destroy the house. That was when I decided to get the soil myself. Transylvanian soil had been my edge, but Bernie over in Saskatoon had grown a mean one last year and he said he only used locally sourced soil.

I checked my watch as I waited in line, 8:45 pm. Good, I still had time before full dark. This was always the most tedious part of Molback's. Their lines were like a gauntlet for gardeners with no willpower. There were always at least two families with kids begging for seeds and a couple of hipsters browsing the pamphlet and magazine racks. And you can't forget the tourists (in a gardening shop, really!) who were always there, exclaiming over the "adorable" bird houses or the "exquisite" hummingbird feeders. I rolled my eyes. It wouldn't be so bad except that they considered themselves to be "in line" as they dawdled near the registers. "What they really need is a fast lane for regulars," I thought to myself, not for the first time.

When I got to the front, I put my bag of starter soil down and handed the woman at the register my seed order receipt. She smiled vacantly and rang up the soil. "That will be $30.72," she said through her mask.

"What about my seeds?" I asked.

She stared at me and looked down at the bag of soil. "Did you forget to get seeds? I can't hold your order for you, you'll need to get them and get back in line."

"No, no!" I said, my voice deepening as I noted how dark it was getting outside. "I ordered seeds to be picked up tonight." I waved at the order receipt. "See? My seeds. I need to get them planted tonight, before the moon rises."

She rolled her eyes then glanced down at the paper I'd handed her. "Alright Mr. Caleeope, calm down. I'll get your seeds."

"That's Calliope," I muttered, but she'd already walked away. "Please hurry," I called after her.

She raised her hand without looking back. I hoped that meant she heard me and was hurrying, but her pace didn't change.

I glanced at my watch again, 9:03 pm. Ugh, moonrise was only an hour away. "Please lord," I prayed to every plant-loving god I could think of. "Please keep the traffic light so I can plant and water these seeds."

A god must have been listening as the traffic on 9 was light and I got home about 15 minutes before moonrise. The sun was down, but I was confident that the moonrise was more important. That's what the plants craved. They would strain for it, grow massive in the moonlight.

I mixed my last vial of Transylvanian blood into the soil, but it wasn't enough. The soil was still dry. Tapping my foot against the bucket, I thought about where I could get some more blood quickly.

I considered snagging one of the noisy chickens from next door, but the coyotes had been decimating them, and I wasn't sure there were many left. The neighbors might notice and object. The other neighbor's dog barked at me as I stood in the twilight. No. That wouldn't work, either.

I sighed. There was no other choice. I pulled out my pocketknife and snapped it open. Before I could change my mind, I held my hand over the bucket of soil and sliced down my palm.

I bit down on my tongue to keep from screaming and squeezed my palm shut, letting the blood drip down into the bucket. When enough blood had dripped in, I grabbed a rag from the potting bench and wrapped my hand. Stirring the bucket of soil was tough with the cut, but I managed, and I dumped the prepared soil into the pots I had set out this morning.

Some people swear that to grow the biggest vampire squashes you need to plant the seeds in a greenhouse on the eve of winter solstice. Instead, I planted them at the first full moonrise before the summer solstice. They didn't have as much time to grow as the greenhouse varieties, but they were hardier and fought for their size more.

One small seed per pot, I reminded myself. The plants would fight one another if they were too close, but too far apart and they'd get lazy, stunting their growth. I laid my pots out in a precise pattern that I'd found promoted optimal growth in the shortest amount of time. I got the last seed into the soil one minute before moonrise, and I wiped my forehead with the rags on my hand.

As the moon rose, I bowed to it. "Thank you for providing my seeds with the moonlight they need to grow and thrive." Then I bowed to the seeds in their potted formation. "And thank you, seeds, for joining my journey to grow the largest vampire squash in the county. I have faith in you."

My hand throbbed, and I cautiously unwrapped the rags to see if the bleeding had stopped. It had, but the cloth stuck to the wound, and I winced as I pulled it off, starting a bit of blood oozing out. I'd need to wash this and wrap it in actual bandages if I didn't want it to get infected.

"They don't need me to watch them grow," I said to myself. It felt wrong to leave them alone this first night. My standard practice was to spend the night with the seedlings, encouraging them with my words and my will. My hand throbbed again. "I'll come back and stay with you after I get this fixed up."

The plants didn't answer.

But I didn't expect them to.

The cut took a long time to bandage because the rag I'd used to staunch the flow had been dirtier than I'd realized in the yard's twilight. Plus, it hurt a lot. Now that I wasn't in front of my seeds, I shouted and cried at the pain from first removing the rags, then rinsing the now oozing cut under cold water, and tweezing out the fibers and bits of muck that had crept in.

"Why don't I keep clean rags handy?" I said to my cat.

She didn't respond. As soon as I had my hands full of bandages and antiseptic cream, however, she was right there, meowing and rubbing against my ankles.

"I should have fed you to the plants," I muttered.

The stupid cat meowed again and marched over to her food dish. She had shoved all the food to the outer edges of the dish and was pawing at the empty spot in the middle, turning her plaintive eyes on me and meowing piteously.

"You are hardly starving!"

This went on for several rounds as I cried and swore over the pain in my hand. But I finally had it all bandaged up, so I headed back outside with a flask and a blanket.

I lay down in my standard spot in the center of the pots of seeds. The moon shone down on us all, and I smiled. This was going to be my best year ever. I knew it. I should have written the exact amounts of soil and blood I'd used so I could replicate it next year.

I dozed off, dreaming of giant zucchini and even larger rabbits creeping through the rustling grasses to eat them.

On the third day after planting, I saw my first shoots. Initially, I was skeptical. The seedlings rarely appear above ground until the fifth day, and I debated calling Molback's to complain that their "sterile" potting soil had been contaminated with wild seed. But as I examined the tiny seedlings with my magnifying glass, I realized I was wrong. These seedlings were my babies, and were more robust than they'd ever been before. I patted the tiny plant with a soft finger and pulled back with a yelp.

"Ouch! No biting Papa," I said, shoving my finger in my mouth. The copper tang of blood was a surprise. "Especially not to draw blood." I patted the dirt beside the seedling, careful to avoid the sharp bits.

Most of the pots with visible seedlings were the ones closest to the middle of the circle. I spent a few minutes rearranging the pots so the others could benefit from that location.

"This may be the best year ever, Diamond," I said to the cat who had wandered outside to beg for more food. I held out my hand to let her sniff it before petting her.

But before I could pet her, she sneezed hard, sniffed my hand and sneezed again. Then she gave me a wide-eyed look and sprinted for the house.

"What the heck was that about?" I wondered. "That cat has always been a spaz!"

The plants were silent on this subject as well.

After a week, the plants had grown so much that I had to repot them. Based on previous years, this was about three weeks early and I grinned at the thought of my giant babies owning the entire vegetation exhibit at the county fair. These beauties might even be destined for state-wide dominance. I hardly dared consider national notoriety, but it was on my mind.

I had taken to carrying a pack of bandages with me. These seedlings were hungry, and they seemed to prefer to poke me. Small nicks and cuts covered my hands and arms where the sharp thorns had scratched me while I watered and weeded. Wearing leather gloves helped at first, but it almost seemed as if the plants were reaching around the leather to get to my skin.

When the plants were two weeks old and I'd repotted them into the garden beds, the leather gloves stopped blocking the thorns. Once I realized that, I threw them back in the potting shed for pruning my roses. I would have to be more careful, and bare fingers allowed me to feel my way through the mulch. Besides, after a while I stopped noticing the scratches, as if the plants had some analgesic in their sap.

After three weeks, the plants were the size of my mature plants from previous years, and they entered the blooming stage. This was fabulous, as the earlier the blooms appeared, the longer I'd have to cultivate the seed pods. My dreams filled with images of giant gourds overflowing the bed of my truck as I drove to the world's fair. I rolled my window down and waved to my friends and family, and we formed a parade of well-wishers driving through town to witness the world's largest vampire gourd.

I watered beneath the leaves of the plants, keeping the buds dry so the flowers would open as soon as possible. The sharp edges of the leaves meant I watered with drops of blood as well as the pure well water that served them best.

Sitting in the center of the garden, in the late afternoon of the twenty-third day after I planted the seeds, I noticed that one of the bright yellow buds had popped open. The flower had soft tendrils at the tips of the petals, almost like eyelashes. The inside of the flower was a bright pink color. This differed from previous years. In the past, the flowers had been completely yellow. I believed that color was to attract the bees they used as pollinators, so the pink inside seemed out of place. I wasn't even sure if bees could see that color.

As I sat enjoying the last sunlight, I saw a paper wasp fly past. These wasps were annoying because they liked to chew on the teak of my garden furniture, and left lines on the wood where they'd gnawed away at it. They didn't normally fly near my vampire plants, so I was curious to see what this one would do.

It seemed attracted to the flower, even though the flower didn't look or act like wood. Maybe it smelled like wood. Or maybe it wasn't a paper wasp. Or maybe this wasp was just an atypical member of its species. I knew all about being atypical.

I watched the wasp drift up to the plant. It was flying low to the ground, then changed course abruptly and sped up. It was zooming straight for the flower.

I stood, holding a magazine rolled up and ready to swat the pest away. But about four inches from the flower, the wasp slowed. It flew up above the flower, then drifted down in a strange dance before coming to light on the edge of the petals. It sniffed around the flower for a second or two, then went straight into the center, aiming for the pinkest part at the base of the flower's cup. As soon as its entire body was inside the cup of petals, the edges snapped closed. The eyelash structures on the edges intertwined, locking the insect in its grave.

I clapped and cheered. This was the first I'd heard of a vampire gourd turning predatory, but I was sure it would lead to larger fruits.

Vampire gourds get their name from their preferred fertilizer source—blood. Most farmers gave them blood in the soil like I did, but a few of us, myself included, liked to provide regular boosters during the growing season. I had a standing order at the butcher for a gallon of pig's blood every week. It had gotten me some funny looks the first time I'd ordered it, but now that I'd won the county fair so many times, they were almost eager to sell me the blood.

As I watched my baby consume the wasp, I wondered if I should increase their blood supplement. I shook my head. It was obvious they could fend for themselves.

"You are going to be the talk of the fair, my beauties," I said, smiling over the plants.

The plants rustled in the wind.

Five weeks after planting, every seed I'd planted had grown at least one flower. I carefully removed all secondary blooms, to encourage the plants to put all their energy into growing that one gourd. The tiny nicks and slight cuts no longer bothered me, and I was used to the faint reddish sheen on them after I'd done my gardening for the day. My callouses were hardening, letting me tolerate the roughness of the petals and the sharp thorns.

Many of my competitors felt that focusing on over one or two plants at once was a mistake. They would plant between five and ten seeds, and ruthlessly cull the smaller plants until only the hardiest were left to grow fruit.

I had found that the plants did better when you kept them in groups. I felt like the plants supported and encouraged each other. At summer's end, I'd choose the largest, most perfect of the plants to enter in the competition.

This year was no different. That's not exactly true. In fact, this year was exceptional in one distinct way—if I hadn't known better, I'd have sworn the plants were working together. I set my garden up in a circular pattern, with my lounge chair in the center, four plants at the cardinal points, eight in the secondary points in a circle around them, and sixteen in the outer circle.

The outer plants had grown larger than the inner plants. This was not surprising. I'd noted that growth pattern in previous years. What was surprising was that their leaves seemed larger and more rigid, almost like shields blocking danger from the center of the plot. These outer plants also had larger thorns, and I had to prune them away from my pathways every day or they would become impassable brambles. They had all bloomed and were nursing a gourd, but these gourds were smaller than the ones on the middle plants. I called this row the shield maidens.

The second row was the nannies. If something dangerous got through the barrier plants, this circle of plants had larger thorns that were almost a foot long and two inches thick at the base. But while they could use these as defense, they seemed more about capturing prey. One morning I came out early, before the sun rose, and stopped at the sight of a rabbit in the garden. I ran to the garden, yelling to scare it away, but almost immediately stopped and stared. The shield maidens had lifted their leaves as if welcoming the rabbit into the circles, and as I watched, one of the nanny plants drove a thorn into the side of the rabbit as it nibbled on a leaf. The rabbit screamed and thrashed, but the plant flung it into the center of the garden, into the waiting pink flower of the central plants.

"Where did that flower come from?" I said aloud.

My words broke the frozen silence that had slid over the yard after the death of the rabbit, and all the plants snapped back to the ground. The shield maiden's leaves lay back on the ground, overrunning my paths. The nanny's thorns were all pushed back up against their stems. And the maternity ward—my name for the four mama plants in the center—all hid their pinkish-white carnivorous flowers.

I gaped in shock for a moment or two, then clapped my hands. "My babies are growing up!" I shouted.

The plants brushed towards me in a wind I couldn't feel, cutting my legs with small, painless cuts as I walked among them, praising their strength and ingenuity.

"You don't need to hide who you are from me," I told them. "I love you, just the way you are."

The plants bowed to me.

"You're welcome," I answered.

I woke at midday in the eleventh week of growth because my skin felt like fire. The sun beat down on me and my precious plants. They loved it, but my pale skin was used to the cloudy days of the Pacific Northwest. What was that yellow thing sending its harsh rays down on me? I pulled my hoodie over my face and sprinted towards the house.

Three steps from the edge of the garden, I stumbled over a small lump of fur. Another bunny had braved the plants, and it had donated its nutrients to the cause. But I looked closer, meat and muscles enrobed this rabbit completely. I poked it with my toe, and it flopped over, showing its white belly. The skin was pale, nearly white, and the rabbit seemed almost a shell. The plants had drained it and tossed the desiccated remains to the side.

Vampire gourds, indeed. I considered my vegetal army. The maternity ward had produced four beautiful gourds. All of them were the size of a house cat, and they shone with a purple hue, like gigantic eggplants. Above the precious gourds were several carnivorous flowers. Now that the plants knew I wouldn't object to their feeding, they had come out of hiding and three of the blooms were large enough to consume a robin or other large birds if they were foolish enough to wander into the greenery.

The spikes on the nanny plants had grown larger, and while these plants had also produced gourds, their fruit was smaller and tucked away in the middle of the plants towards the stems. The nanny plants also had carnivorous blooms, but they were smaller and seemed more suited to catching insects.

The outer row of shield maidens had grown into their name. The largest plants had leaves up to four feet across, and they were as tough as tree bark. They adjusted their leaves like a phalanx of shields—interlocking the leaves to protect the inner plants from most threats. These plants had the smallest gourds of all, most the size of apples. And like apples, the plants held them high off the ground and near the stems that were more like woody trunks. I had thought these plants didn't have any weapons, but as I examined the rabbit, I realized I was wrong. Six inches from where the rabbit lay in my path, the plant had captured another rabbit. A vine had snared it and dragged it partly under one of the shield maiden's leaves. As I watched, a tendril I had thought part of the bark detached and stabbed the still struggling bunny. I gaped in admiration as the bunny relaxed and began rubbing against the plant's bark. I would have sworn the rabbit was in ecstasy as the plant sucked it dry. When the plant finished, the vines dragged the corpse next to the first and left it there.

These plants were amazing. I clapped in appreciation. This reminded me of my poor burnt skin.

"I need to get into the house, out of this sun," I said to the plants.

The shield maidens rustled but didn't part their leaves to let me leave.

"I am not like you," I said. "Strong and vibrant, you revel in the sun. But I am pale and weak, and the sun is harming me." I gestured at my red arms and moved towards the house.

Instead of parting, the leaves of the plant nearest me lifted above my head, blanketing me in cool shade.

I sighed in relief. "Thank you, dear plant," I said, bowing to it. "I'll sit under here for a while until the sun sets or the clouds return to let me work. But your shade is perfect for me to rest and contemplate your amazing growth."

The plants bowed to me, and the wind sounded a lot like laughter as I sat under my prized plants. These plants were the best in the world.

Two weeks before the fair, I stopped sleeping in the house. The shield maidens built a cozy nook out of rabbit fur and composted leaves, and their giant leaves shaded me from the harsh rays of the late summer sun. I looked forward to nights when the moon was near full, as the bright light of the moon shone down on my babies and gave them a silvery glow. Plus, while the moonlight was bright, even at the new moon, it didn't burn my skin and eyes like the sun did, unless I sheltered under the shield maiden's protective foliage.

The cat stopped visiting me in the garden. I suspected that was a good thing, as my babies were not particular about what they snared. Two of the neighbor's chickens had "disappeared" a week ago. I spent the night of their demise clearing feathers from my yard. Thankfully, my neighbors blamed it on coyotes and made comments about getting a dog.

The mamma plants had four huge gourds between them. Each was as large as a pony, and I swore sometimes I could see them growing in the moonlight. The carnivorous blooms grew as well, and the nannies and shield maidens continued to lure unsuspecting animals to their doom. I put up no trespassing and beware of dog signs along the border of my property. I didn't want anyone losing a dog or small toddler and blaming me or my beautiful plants.

I was dozing in the evening sun, waiting for sunset when I could come out from under the shade, when my brother, Ben, showed up at my gate.

"Terry? Terry? Are you in there?" He banged on my gate a few times, then kicked the base in while pulling on the latch. I had shown him the trick to getting it open when I'd first moved here.

I watched him through slitted eyes as he walked up to my porch and knocked on the door. After calling out a few more times, I heard the door open and shut, and I stopped worrying about him. He knew his way around my house, and Diamond liked him. He'd get whatever it was he needed and leave. And I could protect my babies.

"Damnit, Terry! Where the fuck are you?" I heard him yell from the kitchen door out into the yard. "I see you still have those stupid plants." He was walking closer. "Are you out here?"

The surrounding leaves rustled, but they didn't part enough for Ben to see me huddled in my bed. I could still see him through a slit in the leaves.

"Terry?" He was really close now, but still hadn't noticed me. He reached out to push a leaf aside. "Ouch! Damnit! This damn plant bit me! Terry! Your plant made me bleed!" He muttered to himself, "I should burn these suckers to the ground."

I sighed and stood up. Ben would not leave, and he might do something stupid.

"I'm here, Ben. Hold on a second." I slid out from between the leaves, holding my hand over my eyes to shield them from the blinding sun. The leaves caressed my arms, leaving streaks of red behind. Resting my hand on a nearby stem, I smiled at Ben.

Ben had come off the back porch and was standing about three feet away from the maiden closest to the house. He gave off a strange aroma, almost like barbecue or smoked meat. My mouth watered at the thought, and I realized it had been a while since I'd last eaten.

"My god, Terry, you look like shit," he said, leaning towards me to give me a hug. But he pulled back before we connected. "And when's the last time you showered, man?"

Making a big show of sniffing under my arms, I said, "This is what hard work and effort smell like." When he rolled his eyes, I laughed. "Okay, maybe it's been a couple days."

"A couple days? You look like a herd of angry cats ran you over and left you in the mud overnight. Did you sleep out here?" He backed towards the house. "Come on, let's go in and I'll grab us a beer and we can catch up."

I took a step out from under the protection of my shield maiden and winced at the heat from the sun. Hopefully, it would set soon, and I could get to work. But Ben was right. I should clean up and maybe eat something. "Okay, yeah. I'll take a shower, you wanna order something to eat?" My stomach churned at the thought of food, and I rushed into the house before he could answer. The cool air-conditioned room settled my stomach and felt nice on my scorched face. But I wasn't hungry anymore.

Ben had followed me. He had a strange look on his face, but all he said was, "Sure, I'll have something delivered. Any preferences?"

"You decide," I said and headed for the bathroom. Within moments my tankless hot water heater had the bathroom steamy, and I jumped in the shower. I hadn't realized how cold I was until the hot water hit my skin. It woke me up and made me feel almost frisky, full of energy.

Ben knocked on the door. "I need a bandage, Terry. You still keep them in the same place?"

"Yeah, come on in, I'm in the shower," I said over the rushing water. After a second, I heard the door open, and the sharp copper scent of blood filled my nose. "What'd you do, lop off a finger?" I said with a laugh.

"Nah, it was that stupid giant plant of yours. I didn't realize the leaves were like blades and it cut me deeper than I thought."

He rummaged around for a second, then said, "Oh, here it is. Can't see a thing through all this steam. I'll let you finish, then."

The door closed again, and the smell of blood dissipated. I couldn't get over the strange feeling of disappointment as he left. But I was feeling hungry again, and I wondered if it was too late to ask Ben to order a nice juicy steak or maybe a super rare burger. My mouth started watering.

Ben ordered salad. I came out as he was tipping the delivery person. They smelled like antiseptic and diesel, and I wrinkled my nose. The shower seemed to have cleared my sinuses—all the odors and scents were crystal clear to me.

Ben shut the door and jumped when I walked up to him. "Oh! I didn't know you were done. Good timing." He gestured at the bag of food. "Dinner's here."

"You got salad?" I tried to hide the sneer.

"It's got meat in it too. I thought you liked salad." He carried the food into the dining room and set it out on the table. "Get plates and silverware, would you?"

I sniffed the air in the living room but noticed nothing else out of the ordinary. Shrugging, I went into the kitchen to follow orders. "Dishes and silverware as directed, sir!" I said, placing them on the table.

Ben rolled his eyes and dished out salad onto our two plates. He was right, there was steak, not enough, but at least it was something more than just rabbit food. "There's also blue cheese. Eat that too."

I poked at the salad a bit and grimaced at the overcooked steak slices. "Yum," I said, pretending to put a bite in my mouth and chew.

"Just eat it, you jerk," he said. "You obviously aren't eating enough." He waved his fork like a pointer. "You're too skinny. Mom was right."

"Right about what?" I said, shoving a slice of steak in my mouth and talking through it.

"She worries," he said, not exactly explaining.

"So, you're her errand boy?" I raised my eyebrow at him.

"Yup." He speared a cherry tomato and popped it in his mouth. The snap and swish of his teeth piercing the skin made me shiver.

Before I could comment, Diamond came in yelling, as usual. She meowed and waltzed over to Ben as if he came here all the time and demanded he pay attention to her.

"Hey kitty, you're sweet," he said over her cries. Then he stared at me, saying, "Holy crap, dude, did you forget to feed her? She's fucking skin and bones!"

"I feed her," I said, my voice rising. "Her bowl's right over there." I pointed at the counter where her bowl with the food dispenser stood.

Ben got up and grabbed the bowl. "No fucking food, man. That's uncool. You're starving your damn cat! No wonder she ignored you."

He went over to the cupboard where the cat chow was and filled first her bowl then the dispenser. The bag ran out after the dispenser was only one quarter full. Diamond leapt onto the counter and began scarfing down the food.

Ben turned to me. "You need more cat chow." His eyes were sparking, and I wondered if I'd catch fire if he stared at me like that for too long.

When I didn't answer, he continued, "Are you gonna get her more? And where's her fucking water?"

"Water's under the sink," I mumbled.

Ben acted like he couldn't hear me. He marched around the kitchen, first putting out a bowl full of water next to the food bowl, then searching for something else. "Where's your cat carrier? Don't you keep it in the pantry?"

"Yeah, it's on the top shelf in the back."

"I found it." He came out with his prize. "I'm taking your cat. You obviously can't take care of her. She deserves to be with someone who cares about something other than damn plants."

"They aren't damn plants. They are my babies. And you should see them. The mamma plants are doing such a great job this year. The rabbits haven't stood a chance! And the seed gourds are twice as large as I've ever seen them. We're going to win state for sure this year. Maybe even nationals!"

As I spoke, I walked to the window overlooking my patch. The sun was almost down, and the moon made the mamma plants in the center glow.

"You should come see, Ben," I said, turning back to him. He had put Diamond in the carrier with a small bowl of food and was heading out the front door.

"Some other time, Terry," I think I heard him say as the door shut. I wasn't exactly sure as the moon was rising and I could see my babies beckoning me from the deck. I threw down the last of the salad. I'd clean up the dining room later. My babies needed me.

The last rays of the sun burnt my arms as I rushed to them, but the pain disappeared as I rushed under the welcoming canopy of leaves. I reached up to pat the trunk of the largest shield maiden. Most of her blossoms had fallen off early in her growth, and I'd removed all but one or two in my standard pruning. The two on this glorious plant had expanded into gigantic maws capable of engulfing at first small mammals, then birds, and now were almost human-sized.

"You could almost devour me, now, couldn't you?" I purred to the plant. It bent its trunk to lean against me, rubbing my cheek like an affectionate cat. A mild sting told me she'd cut me again, but I didn't mind bleeding for my babies.

I headed for the center of the patch, stroking the nannies I passed and calling out to the smaller shield maidens around the edges. I needed to remember to give some attention to the maidens further away from the house. "You're all my babies," I called to them. "I just need to see how the mammas are doing."

In the center of the patch, the mamma plants had settled on one gourd to focus on. About three weeks ago, I noticed that one gourd was significantly larger than the others. I named it Xavier and assumed he would be the gourd I took with me to the fair. The other three gourds seemed weak. Their skin wasn't as shiny as Xavier's, and they were much smaller than him. I took to sleeping next to him, in the shade of the mamma plants.

One night, after a restless sleep through the heat of the day, I woke to find two of Xavier's siblings were missing and Xavier had tripled in size.

"What happened today?" I asked the plants.

They didn't answer, just rustled their leaves at me. One nanny flung a tendril at my hand, dragging me over to demand blood tribute. I cut my palm and dripped blood over it while considering Xavier. That's when I noticed his stem.

"You're not connected to the western mamma anymore!" I cried out, pulling away from the nanny to rush back to him. I examined the stem that connected him to the eastern-facing mamma plant. It looked like any other stem and seemed to provide him with the nutrients that he needed. But as I examined him, I saw that he now had three connections, not just one. He was connected to the eastern mamma, as I'd noticed. And on the other side, he still had his connection to his original western mamma plant. Plus, he'd connected with the northern-most plant as well. And the eastern and northern gourds were the ones that had disappeared that day.

"Did you eat your brothers?" I asked him.

The gourd shook slightly. It almost looked like it was laughing.

I smiled. "Well, if you're going to get fed by three mammas at once, move closer to all of them." I carefully levered him into the exact center of the patch, so that he was equidistant from the three mamma plants. Then I moved his one remaining sibling over so they were closer together.

I told myself that if the mamma plants wanted to share their nutrients, who was I to stop them? Plus, it wasn't like I *told* Xavier he should eat his remaining sibling. If it happened, it happened.

I ignored the southernmost mamma plant for the rest of the night and focused on the shield maidens and nannies furthest from the house that I'd been neglecting. A few minutes before sunrise, I lay down under a nanny plant, near Xavier, but out of view of the remaining sibling. "Good night, my lovelies," I said. I fell asleep to the sweet sounds of rustling leaves.

Two days before the fair, Xavier was bigger than me.

"How am I going to transport you?" I mused under the leaves of the mamma plants. They had grown in height as well, and their leaves spread like huge beach umbrellas shielding me and our precious Xavier from the harsh light of the sun.

The carnivorous flowers had died a few days before, and the outer-most shield maidens were wilting. But my plants were resourceful and wasted nothing. The nannies used their vines to transfer small animals to the carnivorous flowers, and once they disappeared, directly to the soil around the mamma plants. When the shield maidens drooped, the vines stripped the leaves off and moved them into the center of the garden to mulch around Xavier and his mothers.

I had stopped going into the house at all. My plants needed me here. The sound of the gate opening was surprising, as no one had visited since Ben had come by and taken Diamond away. I didn't open my eyes or get up from my bed under the leaves. The sun was too high in the sky and my skin couldn't take the burning rays.

"Terry! I know you're in there! Come out right now!" Ben's voice echoed through the patch.

"Go away, Ben," I said. My voice was barely a whisper, but I knew my plants would amplify it for me.

"Where are you?" he said. I heard some slashing sounds and he cried out. "What the fuck is going on? Tell your damn plants to leave me alone."

"They'll leave you alone if you leave me alone," I whispered.

The slashing sounds stopped. "I can't leave you alone. The county is going to repossess your land. Your neighbors have been complaining."

"Just two more days," I said.

"I don't think you have two days," Ben said. He sounded closer.

A rustling alerted me that the vines might have one last morsel, and I opened my eyes. Watching Xavier eat was the highlight of my day. But it wasn't the vines.

It was Ben. He'd found my path through the patch and was crawling his way towards me. Leather covered him from head to toe, and on his head was something that looked like a bee hood. His face looked red through the veil, and he was panting in the heat of the patch. Even with the shade, it could get into the 90s by midafternoon, and it was around 3:30 based on the way the canopy had shifted.

"How do you stay out here?" he panted as he reached my nest in the center. "It's like an oven."

"It's not too hot if you were dressed normally." I gestured at his attire.

"Yeah, right, and risk getting chopped into pieces like you've been?" He grimaced as he peered at me through his veil. "No, thank you."

"I'm hardly chopped into pieces. My babies need nutrients." I smiled at Xavier. He was so large that he was more like a green wall behind me. I patted his smooth skin and his barbs cut lightly into my palm, leaving a small smear of delicious blood behind. As I watched, Xavier absorbed the blood, and I sighed with pleasure.

"Gross! How can you do that?" Ben jerked me out of my reverie. "We need to get you out of here."

"No, we need to get Xavier out. He's almost ready."

"Xavier? Who is Xavier?"

I patted the gourd behind me, leaving more smears of blood behind. "My baby. He's right here."

Ben stared at me, his wide mouth reminding me of the carnivorous flowers as they gaped open, waiting to be fed. He snapped it shut and said, "Never mind that. We need to get you out so you can talk to your lawyer. You haven't opened your mail in weeks. The county is going to repossess this land and you and your precious plants are getting evicted."

"None of that matters," I said.

Ben ignored me and grabbed my arm. He tugged, but I was comfortable where I lay in my bed of compost and mulch. The nearest nanny plant looped a vine around his leg and jerked.

"Terry! Call it off!" he yelled at me, but I ignored him. He fell but stood up immediately and swung at the vine with a knife he'd pulled from his pocket.

I winced as the vine tip fell to the ground. But the nanny simply spun more vines around his legs. Then another nanny and another joined in, looping their ropy vines around and around him. His yells and cries grew quieter as the vines surrounded him until all I could hear was the rustling of the leaves.

I wondered if it would take Xavier long to consume him, but the susurrations of the leaves lulled me back to sleep after a moment or two.

The days leading up to the fair were a blur. I heard a commotion near the front of my house, but as it was midday, I couldn't come out into the sunlight, so I ignored it. I spent my days sleeping with Xavier and my nights giving him the sustenance he needed to grow larger than any vampire gourd I'd ever seen.

Blame it on the Pumpkin

It grew harder to walk between the branches of the nannies, and the shield maidens were all dead by the day before the fair. I had given up doing rounds and simply lay with Xavier in the middle of the patch, feeding him and talking to him. He didn't seem to mind. I could no longer measure his size. He'd grown larger than I could stretch my arms up, even standing. Plus, stretching had given me the brilliant idea to feed him more efficiently.

I stripped off all my clothes. The weather was warm and dry, and the mammas kept me and Xavier protected from the sun. I curled myself around the gourd, touching him with every inch of my body. It felt like sandpaper against the more sensitive parts of my anatomy, but I knew he would use every bit that he could. I fell asleep curled around Xavier, murmuring to him, "Tomorrow is our day, Xavier. Tomorrow we win the world."

The sheriff's lights lit up the night on the street outside. In the flashing lights, Murray could see a small yellow house dwarfed by what looked like huge melon plants.

"The property appears abandoned," he spoke into his mic. "Continuing welfare check." The harsh squawk of his radio filled the silent air.

Murray struggled to get the gate open and noticed that the front door appeared to be open and unlocked. He banged on the door, calling out, "Snohomish sheriff, anyone home?"

The door swung open to an empty house. He flicked on a flashlight and walked in, calling out again, "This is the sheriff. Is Mr. Terry Calliope at home?" His flashlight flickered, and he banged it on his thigh. "Why didn't I come do this earlier in the day?" he muttered to himself.

The main room was small and crammed with furniture. Several cabinets dominated the room. The cabinets were packed with what looked like glass mason jars overflowing with dirt and brown liquids. Cobwebs covered the cracks in the ceiling, and an animal was turning the couch into a nest of some sort.

Murray moved into the kitchen and saw a set of dishes on the table, with one that may have had food on it before the animal moved in, laying smashed on the floor. The refrigerator was open and had filled the air with the smell of rotting food, but again, the animal had taken most of it away before it could rot. The only food left in the fridge was in the drawers and in the closed freezer compartment.

Murray opened the freezer and gagged. The smell was overpowering, rotten, and slightly fruity, like a several-week-old corpse. A wave of flies came out with the putrid air.

"I need backup," he said into his radio.

The radio squawked in response, and he continued his exploration of the house, carefully leaving everything where he'd found it and touching as little as possible.

Out the window, the melon plants visible from the front were a thin line hiding what appeared to be the largest gourd he'd ever seen. Scattered around the gourd were the remains of four large plants, piles of hay and straw, and a strange, shrouded bundle at the base.

Murray would say later that it was the spookiest scene he'd ever had to investigate. "There were corpses of dogs and cats strewn around like on some kinda pagan altar," he'd tell his friends when he got really drunk. Then his voice would drop to an almost whisper, "and two dead dudes."

Blame it on the Pumpkin

NASTY OLD B!TCH

By S. P. Mount

In her everyday life, Myrtle Soppingbottom resembled Mrs. Claus. Everyone said so. But, suffering from a flicker of dementia while admiring her Halloween costume in the mirror, her ghastly reflection freaked even herself out.

"Mrs. *Claws*, more like it," she said with a cackle when her pacemaker kicked back in. "And as of now, there will be no more Mrs. nice guy."

She wondered briefly if she could be considered a guy. Then again, it was how the youngsters referred to each other... as 'guys.'

"Back in my day everyone knew that you were either a boy or a girl. There was none of this transgender rubbish. A rough and tumble girl was considered a 'tomboy' and a gentle boy, 'sensitive' or 'artistic.' Granted, though, to call a spade a spade back then saw nonconformists extricated from functioning society and the likelihood of them being incarcerated."

They also called each other 'dude,' but Myrtle was absolutely certain that would not sound right at all if applied to her.

She had been going for a Kim Kardashian look, but being sixty decades too old, it had been too difficult to pull off *exactly*, even she admitted. The love heart cushion stuffed down a tight skirt simply made it look like a rectal prolapse.

"I do look like a nasty old bitch, though. Totes sick. Yes. *Bitch* and *sick*. That's what I'm going for."

And she was certainly sick. But not in the way the youth of the day seemed to have reinvented the Queen's English because of the amount of binging they did on "the Netflix and Chill television shows they call streaming."

"Bloody *trick or treat*," she spat at her reflection. "In my day, we had to say, *the sky is blue, the grass is green; may I have my Halloween*? And then we were expected to sing a song or recite a poem hoping no one would demand we dunk for apples only to be rewarded with a handful of manky monkey nuts.

"Rest assured there will be no such crap given out at my house. No store-bought sweeties... soz... candy... either. Why, when I was a child, our stockings, and not purpose made sacks, were filled with fruit and nuts, homemade biscuits, and cakes . . . Oh, soz... what do the Americans call them... cookies? No indeed, the little darlings will only ever get home baked crap at Myrtle Soppingbottom's house."

And her reflection wholeheartedly agreed judging by the approving nod it gave.

"And don't they know it, Myrts?" it said.

Her natural snow-white hair, usually worn in a bun, intermingled stringy black tresses that reached down to her bottom–or at least where her bottom used to be. The wig had been part of what was called an 'Indian Squaw' costume from back in the sixties before political correctness about describing First Nations women as such became a thing and before saying the word 'thing' in such context was even a thing–such as the children also said.

It had been well used over decades; Myrtle having dressed *as* Thing, Elvira, Morticia and an early Boy George when he was relevant, and of course for an assortment of witches and numerous Sonny and Cher concerts when watching them on television.

In place of her go-to floral patterned smock that displayed the plump and matronly form of the quintessential grandmother figure, but more importantly hid a multitude of sins, pasty, liver spotted flab busted out of what was intended to be worn as a sexy fire engine red-lace bustier that it was no secret had been marketed to an entirely different demographic by someone called Victoria.

"But if anyone tries to body shame me..." She told her BAE, Gladys Featherstone when Gladys expressed shock at Myrtle's costume choice, "I will publicly shame them on the Facebook."

Yes, Myrtle Soppingbottom might have been born early 20th century, but no one could deny she moved with the times.

Trying on the bustier in the shop with flesh dripping like folds of cooking lard, the assistant had told her she looked "totally lit" but whispered to a young woman customer after Myrtle had gone to the dressing room that it made the deluded old fart look like a deflated blow-up castle.

"Like, I'm just keeping it 100, dude," they said.

With her hearing aid on turbo, Myrtle heard every word. How dare the unspecified gendered person think she was one hundred years old? She was only 96.

Surprisingly, though, even if they looked it, not all youth were the same. The young woman quickly jumped to her defence; dismissing the clerk as a hater who was in absolutely no position to body shame.

"Pot calling kettle bright pink, love. You yourself..." she pointed out, "have obvious man-boobs with disgustingly enlarged nipples entirely evident through that cast off *retro* Simon Cowell tank top that shows more pot belly than a celebrity pig, which is undoubtedly the product of a plethora of munchies through constant weed smoking evidenced by your totes gross stained fingers...*ew*...that your passé black nail polish does not detract from *whatsoevs*, girlfriend...like...*hello*...1991 called and wants their hands back for a Michael Jackson zombie vid."

The clerk looked at her simply stunned, but she hadn't finished berating them by any means.

"Plus, those skinny jeans show more toe than a herd of camels at Giza... and I have *no* idea how that can even be possible. Your own butt has obviously collapsed, but I don't know how from all the twerking it does every night up at Bar Capitan Salami... Oh, I *know*, honey... I've seen you... The club is straight friendly now; I go because I am sick of being hit on by grabby dudes when me and my besties just want to trance dance without worrying someone has spiked our mineral water.

"You should be ashamed of yourself. I would never, *ever,* take it upon myself to judge another even privately let alone voice it publicly in the appalling manner you just did to that old lady who admittedly has no valid reason for being in this store."

"You *go* girl?" a large black lady shouted through a pair of crotch-less panties.

Helping Myrtle out of the bustier when she'd come out of the dressing room with it stuck between her bosom and her knees, the girl, exhausted, said there was more likelihood of Myrtle taking possession of the iron throne than finding anything in the store in her actual size, but the black lady suggested that the xxxl bustier might *sort* of work with the seams let out and the back fastened with safety pins.

"That's what *I* do."

"Like, as long as it *is* only for some grotesque Halloween fun, dude, and not, like, for some, like… hashtag… weird kink thing you've got going on with your, like, partner. Because… *gross*… *ew*?" the girl said.

Oh. Myrtle thought. *I am a dude.*

"*Or* you could try the tent department," the clerk took time from another client to say.

"*Ye–ah–no*… We'll leave the 'camping it up' to you, Lady Gaga," the young girl snapped.

Taking the bustier to the counter with renewed bravado and a totally 100 lit dude by her side who had failed to find unicorn horns for some hippy dippy festival in some mucky field or other, Myrtle stared down the clerk's lilac and rose-coloured hair that was undercut on one side to reveal a scalp tattoo in the colours of the rainbow and lowered her glasses onto her nose to read it.

NoH8.

Must be the name of his favorite pop band, she thought.

"I'll take that, and a pack of safety pins, please, dude," she said, tossing the bustier on the counter.

"*Ye-ah, n-o...* Haberdasheries went out of vogue in the last century," they quipped. "I ain't no Mr Selfridge."

"Oh, come on dude. That is so not lit. I mean, don't you punk rockers use safety pins as fashion accessories these days? Put them through your nips, and stuff?"

"*Wotevs,*" they said with a flick of their wrist and rang the ticket through. "Try Woolworths... If you can find a time machine. "And, soz, before you ask, we don't do geriatric discounts. Normally there's no demand."

"You're s-*o* going on YouTube tonight dude," the girl said pointing her phone at him. "I'm judging you *s-o* hard right now."

"Ooh, really?" Myrtle said. "You know... I *s-o-o* intend to be on the tube tonight too."

"Wot... You in one of them Jurassic movies, then?" the clerk said as quick as a whip.

And, surprisingly, the girl laughed too.

"*Right?*" she said.

The precarious ten-inch stiletto heels brought on her vertigo, and Myrtle thought she might very well break her other hip by the end of the night. But she didn't care, it didn't really matter; with what she had planned, the pain would be short-lived.

The only thing left to do was to press on the false nails with skeletons printed on them that had been the last at the dollar store. She'd proudly beat out some whiny little dude to snag those suckers; sending the six-year-old girl flying into a giant box of rubber spiders and bats by shouldering her out of the way in a rather impressive rugby tackle she'd learned old-school style by a lifetime of frequenting post-Christmas sales.

"Yes, Myrtle Soppingbottom put the 'boxing' in Boxing Day before the Google saw people pull punches remotely, insulting each other anonymously on Cybernetic Monday and that one Friday when only black people can buy stuff online."

And not for one minute did Myrtle believe the girl's mother when she said her daughter was only reaching for the glittery fairy wings fluttering from the shelf above and was much too young and too small for the nails anyway. But it was obviously a lie given the grotesque mask the girl planned to wear already in the woman's cart that made Myrtle suggest that her cry-baby didn't need it as she already looked super ugly with her distorted, screaming face full of snot and tears.

"Just keeping it 100. You won't need it, dude," she said to the girl's mother. "Save your money. Although, granted, it is the ugliest mask I have ever seen in my entire life. What is it, a gargoyle?"

"That is not a mask, nor is this a shopping cart, it is a baby sleeping in its pram," the mother retorted.

"Wotevs, Lady Gaga," Myrtle said walking off. "Just trying to help a brother out."

"I am a woman, and I am Korean, you demented old crab!"

Having substituted her dentures with an old, discoloured pair of her dead husband's that put the pagan stones of Stonehenge to shame, Myrtle surveyed the results of her labours around the house that day and smiled.

Every surface was laden with delectable treats splayed underneath black candyfloss spider webs. Candied apples rolled in slivered almonds and walnuts that looked like scabs and warts were always a feast for the eyes.

Her rat-shaped fudge had disappointed though. They looked more like hamsters flattened by their sandboxes. But, placed all over the house, together with chocolate raisin droppings underfoot, the entire place at least looked even dirtier than Gladys' house looked on a daily basis. She had outdone herself.

Soon enough, the doorbell would start chiming and would not stop all night long. Even if she had listened to the merry tune since 1969, she never got tired of it.

You are my sunshine... she sang to Tommy the cat every single time, but turning deaf, perhaps even on purpose, had been Tommy's saving grace. Regardless, somehow, on

Halloween, the normally bright and uplifting tune lent a creepy element to the décor.

"Yup, no generic two-a-penny miniature choccy bars from Costco in my pad, dude," she muttered. "No-siree-Bob."

Unlike how All Hallows' Eve was done in her own childhood, she never asked any of the children to proverbially sing for their supper.

"*Hell* no, *bitches*," she told Gladys and Neris Blenkinsopp in her best African American accent, cricking her neck, trying but failing to emulate that wholly impossible head motion thing she often saw in sitcoms. "I prefer how they do Halloween in America. A simple 'trick or treat' and Bob's your uncle. That will do me nicely, thank you very kindly," she said despite what she always told her reflection every year that wholly contradicted that view.

No, never had Myrtle Soppingbottom's semi-detached home been 'teepeed' for being stingy or pathetic even if Gladys'–the other semi part of it–had. The Soppingbottoms doled out delicacies even to the fattest of children–diabetes a concern or not, and no mind of peanuts either–and even to those children who had been too lazy or much too poor to wear a proper costume such as those that draped a piss-stained sheet over their heads, cut two holes in it and called themselves a ghost. Everyone got their fair share.

She piled lovingly wrapped home-made goodies in colourful greaseproof paper and festooned them with bows of raffia and ribbon and stuffed them into all the children's little begging bags, or sometimes, in the case of the fat greedy ones, pillowcases. And all the while she made sure to admire all costumes whether they were store bought or looked like complete abortions. And she only ever privately judged while imparting encouraging words:

"Oh my, my, dude. You certainly gave me quite the fright," was typical of what she would say to an infant out with his or her or their mummy for the first time dressed as a mummy him, her or themselves.

"If a half assed roll of dirty bandages wrapped around its grubby little face constitutes *being* a mummy," she'd whisper in the ears of Gladys and Neris also there to hand out treats because they were too tight-assed to buy or make their own despite having the same state pension as her and even if Gladys had won a modest amount on the lottery a few years back.

But both wearing hearing aids made her shout it instead. No matter, though, the bounty was worth it to the parents, even if most highly objected to the insult, they wouldn't have to buy their brats any sugary goodies for weeks.

Myrtle tried to be much hipper with the older children who just rolled their eyes at such comments as: "Hey dude, that mask rocks. I totally wet my Depends when I opened the door just like I did the day he was elected president."

Yes, hers was always the first house the children came to with gluttonous anticipation evident in expectant eyes even through a plethora of masks. Putting up with the old hag's stupid comments for a couple of minutes once a year was well worth it. They would be back soon enough to shouting insults through her mail slot and flinging dog poop at her nice shiny windows.

"Ooh, I can't wait. The greedy little dudes will cream their pants when they see what I have to offer," she said rubbing her hands together. "It all looks totally lit."

She had bought up every possible ingredient in the health food store and set to work. With much to do, she hadn't even had a second to open the mail. But what would be the point of that? There was only that one letter from Saint Aloysius' Hospital that would no doubt admonish her for not turning up for treatment and wasting the taxpayer's money as well a possible wasted tea break for the operating surgeon who was always whining about being overworked. An incurable disease, they said. Why *bother*, then?

And, as it was her last hoorah, she had also dished out an extortionate amount of money to the local "artsy-fartsy weirdo dudes from the community theatre" for them to decorate the entire house with more than just some half ass pumpkins and dangly spiders.

"And sure enough, their collective angst has really paid off; my hallways and front parlour have been transformed into a veritable hell that would put even their own sleazy discotheques to shame."

What was the point of all her money then? Having made massive withdrawals from the bank over weeks until her account was cleaned out, she burned what she hadn't spent that day in a big roaring fire in her wood stove when melting bags upon bags of figs and molasses to give her syrup as near as damn it an authentic look of diarrhoea.

Every now and then, one of the safety pins came apart to dig into the lump growing on her back that she at first thought she might have cleverly utilised to go as Quasimodo but thought better of as a mark of respect to the tragedy at Notre Dame.

And anyway, there were the twin dwarfs with humpbacks that always came by dressed as midgets with a woman dressed as Dorothy from *The Wizard of Oz* to consider. She didn't want to body shame them. Although, she was never *entirely* sure if they were actually children or not, since they'd been coming for about twenty years and Gladys had heard the three of them were triplets just out for all the freebies they could get because they were shunned by society, and no one would give them a job. But it didn't matter; all and sundry were welcome to Myrtle Soppingbottom's delectable sundries–that year in particular.

Her medical condition had been getting exponentially worse. The lump on her back growing bigger every day so that those midgets could have gone rock-climbing on it. It wouldn't be long before her body would be completely consumed by it according to the doctor who also inappropriately joked, she thought, that they would have to make a coffin with a hole in the bottom to accommodate her.

Myrtle had thought the doctor had the same tell-tale signs of alcoholism as Neris tried unsuccessfully to keep secret about herself. Drawn, pale pallor with reddened eyes, he spoke with a slur. But still, with a stethoscope around his neck and wearing a white coat he obviously knew his stuff–just as the doctors and dentists on TV commercials did to prove *their* credentials.

He was on coke, or was just overworked, Myrtle decided, or had, at one point, suffered a stroke. Doctors were always tired, always leaving medical utensils inside people. And while she appreciated his frank, no bars held prognosis that she would end up looking like Elephant Man if she didn't get the lump seen to immediately, also saying that even if she did, she was still not long for this world, she decided she would die on her own terms.

Yes, she would go out with such a bang people everywhere would be truly horrified. All Hallows' Eve would never be the same again. Ever.

"Help yourselves dudes, there's plenty more where that came from," she shouted through from the hatch adjoining her kitchen and front parlour.

There was just one more thing to do. Sprinkling a special slice of cake with a white powdery topping, she put it aside for herself later, together with a fillet of fish for Tommy.

"And remember my one and only rule. Don't stuff your faces until you get home," she shouted. "Make sure to be totally lit and share with your mummies and daddies and brothers and sisters."

"Yeah, *that'll* happen," a deep, albeit still breaking voice shouted back.

She looked at the letter from the hospital placed on the bottom shelf of her kitchen island and contemplated for a moment if she were doing the right thing. Should she have opted for treatment? Surely the doctor could not know for sure that she would die if she did. But then she'd had a second opinion; Gladys had agreed completely he would know what he was talking about.

"No, dude," Myrtle mumbled. "You'll totally only end up looking like a walking corpse like some of these little dudes and still kick the bucket. Besides, you have no money left. How would you live now? The damage is done. *Commit*, Cynthia…I mean, Myrtle…*Commit*."

She bent to pick up the letter to trash it making a safety pin pop open and she winced as she felt it prick her lump. A warm oozy substance slowly trickled inside the bustier like the snot inspired lava did from her volcano cake. Strangely, the lump felt much smaller and the bustier much less tight.

Fingering the letter, she again had second thoughts.

"Oh… I dunno, dude, maybe I should read it…."

But the thought of reconsidering was interrupted when a lame semblance of Freddie Kruger sauntered into the room severely insulting her costume and demanding to know where she kept her garbage bags saying he needed something bigger because his sack was already full.

A heavy looking pillowcase swung from what was obviously a broken-off rake shoved up inside a stretched woollen sleeve. His filthy, cracked mask probably belonged to his dad from when the movie first came out in 1984, Myrtle thought, surprised her dementia allowed her to remember that information but not what she had for breakfast that morning, or even if she had any at all.

"Under the sink, dude," she said and tried to high-five his rake.

"Freak," he whispered poking his head under the sink.

That was it. Her mind was made up. No regrets.

"Never mind Mrs Claus, I'll be lucky to make it the two months till Christmastide. What's the bloody point?" she said tossing the letter aside like a Frisbee and Tommy, instinctively made a half-assed effort to go for it.

She patted her wig a little surprised not to feel the snowy white hair that was her crowning glory in old age as its erstwhile thickness and lustre had been when it was jet black for real and after when she went through a phase of colouring it in her forties but stopped because it was much too expensive and needed to be touched up every six weeks.

"Oh yeah. I'm a nasty old bitch," she remembered. "You need to commit Cynthia, I mean Myrtle?" she said–which was what her old stylist had told her about the other dying process.

She stared at Freddie Kruger's bony little butt as he rummaged under her sink and thought she would love to shove the sawn-off rake so far up his ass that it would gouge out any fillings he may or not have at his age. But that would ruin everything. Besides, the little monster would get his dues soon enough. Judging by his haul, he would suffer more than anyone else. Much more.

Finding out she had a terminal disease had come as a huge shock to Myrtle. She had always been the picture of health. Had not suffered a day's sickness in her life–if one didn't count a certain disease contracted from an American soldier back in 1937.

"First my hubby, and now me at only ninety-six-years-old," she had moaned to all the widowed seventy and eighty something year olds on the complimentary old people's hospital shuttle.

"We've all been there, lovey," one of the women had said in an attempt at consolation. "All of us lost our husbands years ago, and all of us are being treated for one terminal disease or another. We're here for you dear. "It's just god's plan."

"*God*? There is no *god*," Myrtle had screeched. "Why save my husband from the sinking of Titanic when he was a baby only to take him away again so soon? Am I *right* bitches?" she said holding her hand high in the air for any to indicate they would high five back if they weren't quite so immobile.

But sympathy was not forthcoming from the hags on the bus; all ogling the young shirtless construction workers who were, in slow motion, building an extension onto the psychiatric ward across from the bus loop.

"All y'all bitches can't possibly know the pain of losing someone after an entire lifetime. I was with my husband way longer than any of you dudes ever were with your dudes," she screeched.

"Fair point, you got to admit," the bus driver, about whom no one was sure, was a man or a woman, said, even the voice providing no indication.

"Taken suddenly at only one hundred years old to the day when a young French maid I hired to pop out a cake gave him a heart attack," Myrtle wailed. "Gone before his time."

"I know just how you feel," the bus driver said getting out of their chair to come and hug her. "I just lost my cat at twenty-two–years old...."

"*Woman*!" most of the other old biddies declared, along with one lady that simultaneously screamed, "diesel dyke."

"While everybody else loses their cats at ten-years-old, or *whatever*..." the bus driver continued, casting dirty looks, "some even get run over when they're kittens... actually... a couple by this bus, mind ya. No, these *bitches...*" they screamed, "can't possibly feel the same kind of pain as you and me, love."

"Soz, dude, what *are* you droning on about?" Myrtle said also ogling the construction workers then.

"*Cray-cray-cray-cray-cray-cray-cray,*" the bus driver sang returning to their seat not looking at the workers once.

"Yes, *diesel dyke, defo,*" Myrtle thought she muttered but maybe shouted, albeit not in the way she knew that one who does not self-identify as such could not just in case she had. "*No... Trans!*" Yes, *that's* it."

"*Cray-cray-cray-cray-cray-cray-cray,*" the bus driver sang again putting their foot down to break the speed limit and hopefully some of the old dears' bones as the bus tossed them around like pennies in an old tin can.

*

Myrtle reasoned that if there were no God, there could be no hell either. There was nothing at all to worry about then by carrying out her evil plan.

"No, the only devil I have to face is the little dude in the living room with two pieces of corkscrew pasta glued to his head that only makes him look like Bambi."

The cunning plot that she literally cooked up all day in preparation of would have her remembered for all eternity. Of that she was absolutely certain.

"Yes, siree Thomas," she told Bob the cat.

Exhausted by the evening's events, handing out horribly delicious treats as well feigned enthusiasm at all the pathetic, half-assed costumes, when the last child left, she lit the roll up cigarette that had fallen out of Freddy Kruger's pocket when he was under the sink, and inhaled deeply.

She hadn't smoked since the war when the American soldier gave her, among other things she would rather forget, a pack of Marlboro and some pantyhose for her favours. But certainly, tobacco tasted vastly different in modern times, she thought. Knocking back gin straight from the cocktail shaker, she switched on the news. Surely, she would have made the local broadcast that only ever reported stories of arson and shoplifters and the like. Maybe even, after what she had done, she would've made the headlines.

A smile crossed her face as she washed down the last of her special cake. Strangely, she wished she had set aside more, as never before had it tasted quite as delicious. But then she felt especially hungry for whatever reason; perhaps because it would be her last meal, she thought. Regardless, she just wanted to munch, munch, munch away.

She eyed Thomas's fish and thought about eating that too, but no, like her cake, it had been especially prepared for him. Thomas needed to eat it if they were going to be together in the afterlife that she did not believe existed.

"But just in case it does, better safe than sorry, eh Tommy boy?"

"*Sure, dude*," Thomas agreed–or at least his meow translating as that in Myrtle's altered state.

Even though the bustier and stilettos both vied to kill her quicker than her illness might ever have done, she had kept them on, admiring her legs as she gurgled down the gin. Being dressed like a hooker was how she wanted to be laid out in her coffin–a note nearby demanding it. Her husband, if an afterlife did exist, would be pleased to finally get his French maid–albeit a nasty old bitch version.

"No one but no one, will say Myrtle Soppingbottom didn't go in bloody style," she said.

"Not bad for an old bird, eh Tommy-boy? I should have worn fishnets in my everyday life. Look Tommy," she said poking him, "how they disguise the varicose veins."

"Whatever you wanna hear, bitch," Tommy appeared to say jumping up demanding his meal.

"Oops, sorry cat dude. Here you go," she said reaching for the plate of fish. "Ooh and here we are, the local news is starting... good timing, dude."

She settled back to watch. Would she have made her mark?

Sadly, every year incidences of tainted treats on Halloween continue to rise. But the number of children affected this year is unprecedented. Numerous reports trace back to a single address in Crackton-Upon-Thames...an address well known over decades as being a Halloween mecca in the community. Indeed, by all accounts, a veritable Halloween tuck shop so that neighbours need not have bothered at all.

An urgent warning goes out to parents tonight. Do check all Halloween bounty. The tainted treats have been baked without sugar, repeat, there is no sugar in these deceivingly delicious looking treats. Cup-cakes have been baked with whole-wheat or rice flour and most are suspected to be gluten free.

"*Hah*!" Myrtle said delighted.

"I showed the greedy little dudes," she cackled just as Tommy fell from the arm of her chair, his neck snapping as his head thudded awkwardly on the metal magazine rack.

"You are my sunshine," she sang half-heartedly straining to pick him up to cradle in her lap.

"*Geezus…* you were a fat lazy little gannet, weren't you Thomas."

It was her turn to keel over next, yet she felt nothing but a strange sensation of delight and more than just a little paranoia. But just then a news flash interrupted the regular news report.

"*Just in, a sixteen-years-old boy was discovered foaming at the mouth lying in a bus stop on the corner of Walnut and Birch. The cause of his condition remains unknown. Sadly, the boy yet unnamed, succumbed to his injuries upon arrival at Saint Aloysius Hospital. The boy was wearing a red and black sweater with a rake inside a sleeve. Halloween poisoning has not been ruled out."*

Myrtle froze just as Tommy's bowels relaxed into her lap.

She looked at the crumbs on her plate and realised what had happened. Freddie Kruger must have swiped the cake she had reserved for herself. The one sprinkled with an entire prescription of ground-up sleeping pills intended to make her slip away quickly and quietly, together with Tommy. Yes, that was why she was wide-awake. Her suicide cake had really been one of the gluten free sugarless ones, which, nonetheless had tasted delicious for some reason.

She remembered putting her cake aside on the countertop when Freddy came into the kitchen and distracted her, telling her she looked like mutton dressed as lamb and that she wouldn't even make it on to that old lady porn site, GILFs. One of the other cakes, with a ton of baking soda made to look like icing sugar, was obviously what she had eaten.

"*Sugar*?" she said ironically. "I only meant to disappoint the little brats by making them eat tasteless treats. I didn't mean to kill anybody."

"Oh, but ya did, Blanche, ya did," a signed portrait of Bette Davis that had been her husband's pride and joy from when he had met her on Brighton Pier seemed to come to life to tell her.

She panicked. There were no more sleeping pills and no time to think of how else she might commit hari-kari. She had not shaved her legs in years, and with her husband gone there were no razor blades in the house to slit her wrists with let alone a samurai sword, except a plastic one from when he had dressed up as a Power Ranger on one of their role-playing nights.

It was too late. The sirens were getting louder and despite the most expensive blackout curtains from the Amazon, her living room transformed into a den of iniquity with the blue and red lights of police vehicles flashing outside.

"Oh dude, I'm in deep shit," she said to Tommy's carcass. "People will judge me so hard."

But Tommy only slithered down her legs by the stickiness of his body fluids; his progress impeded by his claws catching in her fishnets as she tried to stand.

"Tommy... Wake up... *Tommy* . . . What's wrong, dude?" Are you having a catnap?"

When Myrtle was transferred from the psychiatric unit where she was surprised to see the consulting physician who had diagnosed her lump, also admitted as a patient–and, in the nurse's words, one of the more 'cray-cray' they had ever known–her letter from Saint Aloysius' hospital had been laid opened and laid on her prison cell bunk, adding insult to injury when she read it.

Dear Old Mrs. Soppingbottom,

We write to inform you that there has been a most unfortunate error. An impostor posing as your consulting doctor was, in fact, a patient escaped from our psychiatric ward due to the renovations that temporarily compromised security measures. Even the hot construction workers who were too busy wiping sweat from their chests and pouring bottles of water over their heads and shaking them in slow motion did not see anyone leave through the gap in the wall they created.

But there is exceptionally good news, while at this time, the patient, and three others are still at large, we are pleased to be able to inform you that the lump on your back is benign; in fact, it is just a nasty old boil that got out of hand, probably from a flea bite from a pet, like a cat, a dog, or an iguana. Your local GP will be able to administer a local anaesthetic and lance it at your earliest convenience, or you could just stick a pin in it... your choice. No need to worry at all whatsoever, though.

Further, taking your medical records into account, we have no doubt you will live an exceedingly long and healthy life–you may even break the world record currently held by some old crone who still works in a paddy field somewhere outside of Shanghai. It's impossible to tell anymore if it's a man or a woman, or even an alien being, but still....

Sorry about the little mix up we hope you understand that these things do happen from time to time... did you ever see that Leonardo di Caprio movie... the one where he pretends to be a pilot and a doctor and stuff? If not, watch that. It will explain nicely how these things can happen. (Sorry, I cannot remember the name of it.)

Finally, as a gesture of goodwill, and absolutely nothing to do with your surname, please find enclosed a voucher for £5.00 off a colonic irrigation valid for one month from the date of this letter–21st October–although the clinic is in Ireland.

Again, extremely sorry about the mix up, old Mrs. Soppingbottom, please accept our sincerest apologies.

Sincerely,

A real doctor at St Aloysius Hospital.

Ps: Happy Halloween.

Blame it on the Pumpkin

FLOCK OF BADB

By S. P. Mount

Given what day it was, Wilhelmina Lee desperately hoped the cacophony of squawking that abruptly cracked the icy silence of night was about a bum lying dead in the alley. There were hours yet until dawn.

"Please let it be someone who overdosed," she whispered jumping out of bed. "Or died of hypothermia."

Tentatively raising the Venetian blind to her bachelor suite window and peering down into the street, her heart sunk. The Hitchcockian scene before her was nothing quite as normal as a poor unfortunate's eyes being pecked out.

A smattering of snow diffused by the orange light of the perpetually flickering lamppost outside her window appeared otherworldly. But then she spied them. Amid veils of undulating mist, ominous silhouettes against a tempestuous Michelangelo sky, lined telegraph wires, rooftops, and fences that looked even more sinister for the ragged icicles dripping from them like the fangs of salivating ogres. The Conspiracy had come for her–and not to sing 'Happy Birthday' either.

"*Shit!*"

The presence of the ravens en masse couldn't possibly be coincidental. She knew then that the bizarre content of the disturbing letter she'd received on her eighteenth birthday exactly three years before, and which she had only half-heartedly scoffed at as being ridiculous, had to be true.

Releasing the cord, she let the blind slam onto the windowsill and knock over a small spider plant before tugging the drapes together forcefully as if they would be any kind of shield. A cold sweat permeated her pores like garbage water seeping from a garbage bag. The room spun. Her knees buckled. And for a grand finale, she vomited on the shag pile rug she'd treated herself to for her birthday. Her only gift.

She had lain awake since midnight–the stroke of which marked her 21st. Sleep was impossible, and not just for the usual blare of Saturday night traffic mingled with the cheerful banter from the drunks leaving the pub at the end of the street–louder than normal for being the night before Halloween. Before the day was over, she might very well become even more of a freak of nature than society already perceived her to be.

Her father's letter had obviously been hastily written; the handwriting akin to what Sister Pauline at the orphanage would colorfully describe as a "sparrow scrawling in shite." And she had not been far off the mark.

From her "presumed dead" father, disappeared on his own 21st on the day she was born, it outlined vague details of an ancient curse cast upon their lineage and a warning that she should prepare for the stark reality of her existence. She should believe, as he had not, the curse was real.

'The flock will escort you into the fold upon your twenty-first birthday,' it read. 'As they come now for me.'

A snapshot of an incredibly handsome man, donning what looked to be a beak, was included.

"*Freako*!" Wilhelmina said. "No wonder my mother went doolally and topped herself."

It was a sick joke by a raving lunatic. Obviously. Unsettling, though, in that a parent would think to premeditate such a nasty deed for their child years into the future. Nonetheless, with the convenience of ancestry websites, the letter sparked Wilhelmina's interest in finding out more about just what kind of crazy she came from exactly.

Months of research turned up extraordinarily little. But that alone spoke volumes. There was no record of a single member of her paternal lineage beyond the age of twenty-one. Shockingly, she discovered her father, as were his mother and her father and so on as far back as she could trace, were all born on October 31st at 12am precisely. Those odds were impossible by any stretch of the imagination and so served to give credence to his letter.

Spitting her DNA into a tube and registering the results on a genealogy site turned up hordes of distant maternal relatives, but only one paternal–a fourth cousin, who went by the handle, 'Ravenhook'.

"Well, I hope *that's* just a bizarre coincidence," she muttered to Snort, her elderly cat.

While Irish and Scottish accounted for 38% of Wilhelmina and Ravenhook's DNA, with another 12% varying, they both had 50% listed as 'unidentifiable'.

It was unfathomable. GEDmatch insisted the sample was compromised, stopping short of suggesting she must hail from a lost tribe in the Amazonian, but suggested she resubmit using the complimentary kit they sent. But in her heart, Wilhelmina knew it would not change a thing and for a laugh, sent Snort's DNA sample off instead.

Ravenhook had been quick to email asking her name, her birthday, where she lived, were her parents alive and suchlike, and she'd written five pages in 10-point font, single-spacing detailing the entirety of her life, woes, and all, signing off with sincerest hopes of meeting up for a family reunion:

'... *or at least, a union, lol*,' she added together with a row of laughing Emoji and love hearts.

She waited a year and sent umpteen chaser emails until finally realizing, as usual, she'd come on way too strong. Regardless she'd attached her best Snapchat selfie, with hindsight it was probably not a good idea to use the bunny rabbit filter to disguise her true ugliness. Her emails contained everything Ravenhook needed to know to avoid her–just like everyone else did.

Ravenhook's one and only initial email did not disclose any personal information whatsoever. If it were not for the DNA that proved they were connected, she'd suspect someone was trying to steal her identity.

"But then, even I don't want *that*."

Consulting the medical records at the hospital where she'd been born, apparently, hers had been an unusual birth. And, given what she discovered, one for the record books. It also lent credence to the story Sister Pauline used to delight in relaying to the other children, in that when baby Willy arrived at the orphanage, she thought social services must've got lost en route to the zoo:

"Seriously, dudes...," she'd laugh, "I didn't know whether to put her in a cot or in with the guinea pigs."

A midwife's appendix to her birth record revealed the truly bizarre nature of it, serving to confirm that Wilhelmina could no longer dismiss her father's letter entirely:

'Cocooned in a shell-like membrane, covered by a soft dark down, at 2Ibs 3oz, in the absence of any contraction, Baby Lee plopped from the birth canal in a comparable manner to an egg being laid.'

Wilhelmina considered Ravenhook might be in the same boat and wrote as short an email as her first was lengthy.

'Hey Ravenhook,

Sorry to bother you, AGAIN, but can you tell me if you actually expect to become a raven?

"*Hah*!" she exclaimed to Snort. "If they don't know what I'm talking about and didn't think I was cray-cray before, *that'll* do it."

But then she had an epiphany.

"*OMG*! Snorty... That's *it*! They must have transmogrified; maybe they were born a year or two or so before me. They *can't* write back!"

And, as she expected, still there had been no response.

The pub had been packed to the rafters that night; a surprise party being held in honor of Dain, the regular bartender, who shared Wilhelmina's birthday. He had arrived for work pissed off because his boss had refused to give him the Saturday night off for his own 21st celebrations. But it was Dain. Everybody loved Dain–including Wilhelmina, who, more accurately, was completely obsessed by Dain. It had just been a ruse to get him there, his boss in on it the entire time. He was Dain. Naturally, there would be a party for Dain. They had decorated the entire pub for Dain, inside *and* out.

Wilhelmina only ever usually went to the pub to ogle him. Clad in his casual 'uniform' of a black T-shirt and tight black jeans, his lithe body moved slickly up and down the length of the bar like a sleek black panther. According to her diary, his 6ft 4in height was as supple as a never-ending stick of delicious licorice while succulent blood-red lips, redder for the pale of his skin, lent him a delectably 'vampiric' look.

His quick-witted rapport with the female punters was always delivered with a blinding smile and a wink from grey black eyes that made Wilhelmina weaken at the knees every single time.

"*He–y*, beautiful . . . What's your pleasure?" he would quip making them gush, their tips all but being stuffed down his front and into his waistband.

"*You*, Dain. *You're* their pleasure," Wilhelmina muttered more than once if no one sat on the stool next to her–which was more often than not.

He had never used any such compliment on Wilhelmina, though. Either, obviously unable to convincingly affect what was mostly insincere compliments to make even the ugliest bug feel special, or the fact he *kind* of knew her from having been in the same grade at school.

Nonetheless, Wilhelmina was content with a subtle acknowledgement; the tilt of his chin and a curt, *S'up*. The exchange at least afforded the opportunity for her to stare directly into his face instead of zooming in on it as well other parts of his anatomy from the photos she'd sneaked when pretending to take selfies from her side of the bar.

She hadn't expected Dain to be there. Not on the Saturday eve of his 21st, and because celebrating such a momentous occasion on a Sunday just wouldn't cut it for a popular, beloved guy like Dain–just as it wouldn't the Halloween revelers before *actual* Halloween who came decked out. But, given she'd gone to mark her own auspicious occasion, telling Snort that only losers stayed at home on their 21st let alone a Saturday night, Dain's presence, as well his party, was a bonus.

Outside of getting to gawp at him from her side of the bar, taking as many photos and videos as she liked because cameras flashed everywhere, it was easy to pretend his friends celebrated her too when they broke into a rendition of 'Happy Birthday', mumbling her own name as they reached the 'Dear Dain' part. Pathetic, she knew.

"Still, better than getting Alexa to do it at home," she mumbled into her drink.

Despite she'd gone to school with many in attendance–most of the girls in slutty cat costumes and the guys in whatever clever get-up punned the world of politics and movies–Wilhelmina, as usual, sat alone. Dain had acknowledged her, though, uttering his usual *S'up*, but also completely surprising her by having a bottle of Prosecco sent over–even if the barmaid did slam the bottle down together with a single glass as she rolled her eyes: "From Dain," she said. "For, like, *whatevs*." Outside of Dain sticking his tongue down her throat, it was the best birthday gift she could ever have hoped for.

Exhilarated, Wilhelmina had no idea Dain even knew they were birthday twins and, peering through a couple of fat ass girls surrounding his table, she stuck an awkward 'thumbs up' at him.

He himself glanced at her almost obsessively throughout the night, though; a smoldering, pensive look on his face, his furtive glimpses inducing body trembles and absolute wanton desire the drunker she became.

It didn't make any sense, not with the slew of attractive girls fawning over him. She knew he could not possibly fancy her. She was *Willy the witch* after all, even with the unibrow threaded and highlights that, even if they wouldn't lift to a desirable level of blonde, at the very least diffused her thick mane of blue-black hair that would put the English mastiff she groomed at work to shame. The bangs were a massive mistake, though, she knew; her nose protruded exactly like the beak in her father's photo.

She thought of how he could take his pick of any girl in school; the rumor being he had made it his mission to bed every girl in the 12th grade. She had been the obvious exception–pointed out, much to her mortification on the night of his, and indeed, *their*, 17th birthday–even if no one else knew it was hers. When a dare was made for Dain to hook up with Willy the Witch at his birthday slash Halloween party, she'd only heard about through eavesdropping in the dressing room at school, self-admittedly, she'd held her breath, hoping he wouldn't forfeit.

☙

The clerk at the liquor store initially refused to even look at her fake I.D. saying: "There's absolutely no need ma'am," when she insisted on waving it in his face and obligating purely under duress.

The Pernod was exactly the Dutch courage and the inspiration needed to pull together a makeshift costume. "*Always* the best kind Snorty-boy," she'd slurred admiring herself in the mirror before trotting off on 8inch heels to the street on which Dain lived fifteen blocks away.

It was not long before the attention focused on her; the girls sniggering at how tragic she looked, the boys, mildly attracted, confirmed by the one guy shouting: "Nice legs, shame about the face," while another quipped: "That's what *these* are for," blowing up a brown paper bag and busting it.

"Go *on*, birthday boy," someone else shouted, slapping Dain on the back. "You've made it your mission to lay every other girl in the 12th grade... take Willy the witch for a test ride on her broom. I *dare* you."

As he stared, trying to work out exactly who Wilhelmina had come as, the room fell silent— not least of which because the playlist on

Spotify had ended abruptly. And then came the chant:

"*Dain-o... Dain-o... Dain-o....*"

His gaze, fixed on Wilhelmina, appeared to contemplate fulfilling the dare until his countenance, speaking volumes, finally said what his mouth wasn't willing to: "Like... As *if.*"

The room had groaned in harmonic disappointment as Wilhelmina–dressed as a hybrid of Kim Kardashian cum Morticia–hastily left; the oversized heart-shaped pillow shoved up her tight skirt left behind in place of a glass slipper–the cushion, a problem since Maple & 3rd.

Their seventeenth was a night Wilhelmina would rather forget, but, given his attention towards her in the pub on their 21st, she couldn't help but wonder if *finally,* he was going to make good and complete his mission... for what else? But no, as usual, Wilhelmina Lee had gone home alone as she watched Dain be dragged off on the shoulders of his buddies into an Uber to continue partying downtown.

"Alexa... sing me Happy Birthday please," she whimpered upon closing her door.

"Sorry...I don't know that one," Alexa said.

The crack of a BB gun caused the tumult of what sounded like hundreds of fluttering wings sounding as if the FBI and the military had descended upon the street. But no, nothing quite as normal; the pre-dawn sky had sprung to life by the conspiracy fleeing; the birds dissipating to conspire elsewhere as John Harrison's voice could be heard loud and clear from across the road before his window slammed shut:

"Fucking hell, man, biblical or *what*?"

But Wilhelmina knew they would be back. Paranoia consumed her even more so than the time she'd stumbled across Sister Pauline's stash in a chalice and smoked a big fatty in her small chapel's vestibule.

Made sure the ravens were gone, she climbed back into bed and pulled her duvet up over her head to prepare for a good cry when the back of her hand snagged the cotton. Tentatively stroking the skin, she was aghast that it felt like the soft wire brush she groomed dogs at work with. Tiny, sturdy prickles.

"Alexa, turn on bedroom light," she mumbled almost in tears, fearing the transformation had already begun.

"Sorry... I don't know that... try going into...."

Wilhelmina groaned, mumbling she should have gone for the Google version of a digital assistant.

"Alexa, *stop*! Useless *bitch*...," she muttered reaching over to switch on the lamp manually.

"*Charming*!" Alexa said.

"Yeah... you understood *that*, though... *didn't* you... *bitch*?" she said, and Alexa simply made a sound that meant she would refuse to engage further.

The sudden wash of an amber glow from the Edison bulb in the bedside lamp seemed alluring. The urge to call out as if announcing the dawn alarmed her. Closing her eyes, Wilhelmina prepared herself for she knew not what.

Tiny dark bristles spread from her wrists to the cuticles of the slender fingers Sister Maria always remarked were perfect piano fingers while Sister Pauline quipped, they were long and spindly like E. T's but at least she only needed one hand to reach the high and low keys of the keyboard simultaneously.

"*OMG*!" Wilhelmina screeched surprised by the sudden raspy pitch of her voice as she stared at her hands in horror; her fingernails, claw-like, as if pressed on for Halloween.

It'll take more than even the dog clippers I use for the English mastiff to trim these suckers, she thought.

Nonetheless, still hands, she wailed into them feeling at least her face was as normal as it had ever felt–which was, according to Sister Pauline, "An unusually jagged bone structure set under a perfectly symmetrical cranium more suited to a cavewoman." Her eyes, set at the sides of her face, had "one going to the store and the other coming back with the change."

A tapping on the windowpane momentarily startled her. *A branch from the tree outside*? The City Parks Department hadn't trimmed it in years. Wilhelmina complained about it, along with the flickering lamppost since the day she moved in simply to exercise her right as a rent-paying citizen even though the City paid her rent.

The howl of a sudden wind made her lamp flicker as if it were a candle; the branches sometimes encroaching the power lines right outside her window on which a single raven used to perch to stare into her room before becoming the main target of John Harrison's BB gun. She flopped on her pillow contemplating her predicament. Should she hand herself over to the world of science or succumb and fly away with the flock?

"I don't want to be a fucking bird," she muttered.

She felt her one eye blink slowly after which she could simultaneously see the ceiling fan and the pillow behind her.

"*Ohmigod. Ohmigod*. That is so fucking creepy. No... no... no... no; this *can't* be happening."

A sudden crash at the window was obviously more than just a branch swaying. She sat upright, petrified.

"Alexa... is it windy?" she asked more to hear another voice than anything else.

"Currently it's breezy at 4.7 kilometres per hour. Tonight, expect more of the same."

Wilhelmina had no idea if that was a slight or strong wind and wished Alexa had just said 'yes'.

The crashing came again, this time a distinct cracking sound made her jump, and a raspy little scream escaped her throat. She scrambled to get out of bed and twitched at the curtains like she did around the time Dain sauntered by whistling at the end of his shift. Mostly he was alone, but at weekends it was not unusual to see a bar trollop or two hanging onto him like lichens to a gravestone. He had the most endearing swagger so that she thought his super long legs surely had to have the slightest knock-knees for his entire body to sway such as it did. Deformity or not, it was hot.

A deafening thud brought about the distinct crack of glass, and she backed off tentatively pulling back the drapes only to see the glass spattered with blood.

"*Omigod... Omigod....*"

And then she saw it; coming in for another dive-bomb, a hefty looking raven.

"Go away... go away... *shoo, shoo,*" she said waving her arms suddenly feeling she might take flight herself.

The bird smashed through the pane to flop on the floor, a bunch of dried leaves stuffed in its beak. Wriggling upright, it fluttered around the room and perched on top of the wardrobe before dropping the leaves at her feet.

Snort appeared at the bathroom door emitting a growl more suited to a German Shepherd as his arthritic body attempted to adopt stealth mode. Seeming to stare at Wilhelmina for a moment, the bird hopped onto the windowsill and burrowed its way out with a final backwards glance.

Wilhelmina shuddered.

"Oh Jesus, Mary and Joseph, that's so fucking creepy," she said channeling Sister Pauline when she'd called in Father Murphy to perform an exorcism on little Sally O'Brien after she frothed at the mouth and spoke in tongues before it was discovered she had overdosed on what she thought was a bag of candy found in the vestibule.

Wilhelmina focused on the leaves.

"Alexa... what does a bunch of dead leaves represent?" she asked subconsciously.

"Sadness," Alexa said, the voice sounding relatively sad itself.

"Alexa...how long do ravens live?"

"The lifespan of a raven is forty-four years."

"*Daddy*?" Wilhelmina whispered at the window as if she had ever said such a thing before in her life.

Or maybe its Ravenhook, she thought. She did give all her personal information in an email to a total stranger.

With her eyes feeling like camera shutters on slow exposure, she searched the street outside in vain silently freaking out that she could simultaneously see into the bathroom behind her. Snort, back hunched, hissed and growled, and given his unique disability, snorted when a swift, dark shadow whooshed by. Wilhelmina stepped back, the tendons emerged from her toes, wiry and curled, snagging the rug. Her phone pinged; the push notification of her Gmail kicking in for the very first time ever.

"Oh... what the *hell* is going on?" she wailed but then noticed the email address.

"*Ravenhook*?"

Almost ripping the curtains from their rod, she screeched when Snort, seizing the moment, clawed her ankle before disappearing back to curl up in the bathroom sink before the loud thumping of Mrs. Biggar's cane from the other side of the wall admonished her.

"Fuck off," Wilhelmina screamed. "Just *fuck* off."

"*You* fuck off you… fucking *witch*… and shut the hell up. It's after three in the morning."

The finger Wilhelmina gave was more passionate for the witch's claw it had started to look like before trying to employ it to open her phone with the passcode, her fingerprint no longer a fingerprint.

'Willy,

Text me on 778 899 1158, it's like, urgent.

Dain.'

"*What*?" she said. "*Dain*?"

Despite her excitement, she was disappointed; people only called her Willy being mean.

'Dain? Wtf? Yes, I'm home… what up?' she texted. That's what they say, isn't it… what up? But the phone rang seconds after she sent it.

"*Willy*?" he said, his voice breathless. "I need to… *like*…hook up with you…like right *now*."

It was everything she ever dreamed of. Dain barging into her bedroom in the middle of night. *But why?*

It's true, she thought, *he does want to complete his mission. He was really wasted in the bar earlier.*

But how could she possibly invite him into her bed? Her legs had started sprouting feathers never mind her claw feet could snag up a Chihuahua.

You could say it's a Halloween costume, a little voice in her mind that desperately wanted a night of passion with Dain muttered. *It's your last night as a human, Willy. To hell with it.*

But Dain was Ravenhook, therefore, a relative. Her mind spun as she weighed the morality of sleeping with a fourth cousin.

"*Shit!*" she said. "It's not just the ravens conspiring against me, it's the fucking universe."

"*What?*" Dain said.

"Oh, *sorry*... nothing. But...*you*'re Ravenhook?"

"I'll explain. I promise. I just...like...need to see you like...*right* now, Willy."

"It's Wilhelmina."

"Oh...*dope*. But like...I need to see you. Is that... like... *your* light on up there?"

Wilhelmina eyed the lamp, confused.

"You know where I live?"

"Well, like...*yah*. You told me in your über long email yonks ago...and anyway...like...I always see you spying on me when I finish my shift," he said laughing. Your face is quite distinctive...even at a distance."

She felt mortified. She thought she had been so furtive in her stalking endeavors.

"*Willy*... uh... I mean Wilhelmina?"

"Um...*yah*...it's my light."

"Okay, open the window...I'm coming in."

"It's four stories *up* Dain. Are you *sure* you know where I live?"

"Oh *yah*. Just open the window. I'm like...out front," he said and hung up.

"What the *fuck*?" she screeched quickly looking around at numerous photographs, as well the giant poster of him on the wall opposite her bed. "*OMG*!"

Hastily turning the frames over, ripping the poster from the wall, she bunched her bra and knickers, discarded on a chair, under a cushion, stopping dead when an ear-piercing scream resounded from the other side of the wall, quickly followed by an urgent rat-a-tat-rat on her window.

"How the *hell*...?"

Drawing the blind, a bare-chested Dain floated like a bad boy angel, a regal black crest adorning the top of his head. And just as Mrs. Biggar had, Wilhelmina almost fainted at the sight of him. The blades of his shoulders, broader than they looked under his black T-shirt, sported magnificent black wings that fluttered almost in slow motion. He flashed a brilliant smile.

"*Fuck* me!" she muttered under her breath. "Have I *died* and gone to heaven?"

He was even more beautiful than beauty itself.

"Open the window, Willy," he urged. "Before...like... the old woman next door comes to and...like...realizes she wasn't having a wet dream."

Beside herself, Wilhelmina pulled up the window and he wriggled in, his glorious wings barely making it through. He smelled of Axe body spray and a little sweat that defied the deodorant's claims.

"The old bag's light was on too," he said. "I thought it must've been one of yours."

"No, I only have the one," Wilhelmina said completely mesmerized. "Except for a fake window in the bathroom."

Snort appeared, hunched his back, and rubbed against Dain's legs purring softly.

"Oh, what a *cute* pussy."

Wilhelmina closed her eyes and inhaled deeply.

"Of *course*," she muttered. "Even the most obnoxious pussy in the world loves the great Dain."

"Sorry, *what*?"

"Nothing.

"*Dain*...what the actual *fuck*...?"

"I could like... ask you the same thing... *Mrs. Claws*," he said indicating the talons protruding from her toes not at all surprised.

"*Um... uh*... it's a Halloween costume?" she attempted weakly.

"Yah... and *I'm Batman*," he said in the way people mimic the famous tagline.

It transpired Dain had been prepared for the eventuality of transmogrifying into a raven for the entirety of his life. His mother had worked *her* entire twenty-one years to find a way to break the curse but failed; her mission continuing through his father and grandparents.

"Like...once upon a time in Ireland...a witch named Badb took the form of a raven and cursed one of our mutual ancestors...Aongus of the Birds...for...like...
murdering her two sisters, Macha and Anad. Together, the 'Three Morrigna'...as they were known...were responsible for bringing about...like...that situation where no one has anything to eat...and...."

"*Famine*?" Wilhelmina said.

"No...I had a curry after the party."

Her eyebrow involuntarily raised.

"Anyway, that thing...and floods...and other shit," Dain said obviously struggling to recount the tale.

Wilhelmina sat entranced, not just by the story, but the fact that he suddenly sounded like a clueless teenager and not the smooth-talking heartbreaker she was accustomed to from the bar.

"One morning Aongus awoke to two golden eggs on his pillow, which, when cracked open, contained black hearts that were...like...beating. Badb...like...fluttering above them like a bat out of hell...cast a spell upon him, meaning his descendants would be born on...*Oíche Shamhna*?" he said appearing to question if he had pronounced it correctly and Wilhelmina's expression told him she was clueless. "Irish for 'Halloween,' my Gran said.

"*Anyhoo*...on...like...reaching the age of maturity his descendants would transform into ravens and...like... flock off," he said grinning at his pun. "Oh...and the females would not be bestowed with beauty...the good-looking...like...*genes*...I guess...transferred to the males."

"So...obvs...*like*...the women got all the *brains,* then?" Wilhelmina quipped, annoyed at how dumb he sounded.

But he was the darkest of princes sitting on *her* bed. Beggars could not be choosers.

"So, *your* mother wasn't beautiful?" she said.

"*Nah*. From the pictures I saw, she looked kinda like you."

"Gee...*thanks.*"

"Just keeping it one hundred, dude."

"*Fair,*" she said, thinking nothing was ever fair at all.

"So... what we do?"

"The only way to...like...break the curse...is when human ravens mate on the day of transformation. So... we have to...*like*...hook up. I *guess,*" he smiled.

Wilhelmina's body fluids positively bubbled at the prospect unless her insides had started to regurgitate the prosecco.

"I mean...*Dain*...like...I *get* it. But *you* look so snatched. Me, though...how can you possibly get *this* aesthetic?"

Really, Willy... are you really trying to talk yourself out of this? It's Dain...new and improved with fucking wings!

"I think it's like...kinda *hot...actually,*" he said. "I've never done it...like...with an *actual* chick before."

Wilhelmina rolled her eyes, but his uncultured candor scorched her thighs until she felt a protrusion on her nose.

"*Shit,*" he laughed. "You're getting a beak. We better hurry...I'm...like...good to go now," he said indicating his crotch with a cheeky smile.

Looking into his lap, Wilhelmina's stomach flipped like the time Sister Pauline shoved her off a cliff bungee jump before she was fully prepared.

"*O–kay*," she squawked. "Alexa...turn off the light."

"Alexa...turn *on* the light," Dain said. "And...like... don't listen to Willy no more."

Anymore. She wanted to correct him by saying, suddenly understanding why some people did not want their lovers to speak. But he was beautiful, and his stunning face loomed down onto hers just as she had always imagined until her beak popped out proper, stabbing him in the eye.

"*Ow*! *Fuck*," he screamed.

"Oh... *sorry*."

"I guess there'll be no kissing then. *Dope*," he said unbuckling his belt.

Wilhelmina, shaking with anticipation, could hardly believe it. Dain was about to take her; she could not wait to feel his body against hers...*in* hers. But then he sat up, rubbing his crotch frantically.

OMG. He's repulsed, she thought seeing the splendor of the lump that caught her breath from only moments before had completely disappeared.

"Oh *shit*!" he said. "It's *gone*."

"It's *okay*, Dain," she squawked rubbing his wings. "It happens, just give it a minute."

"No...I mean...like...it's *gone*, gone. My...*penis*...has disappeared. I think I must be turning into like a...like a...*lady* raven."

"Oh... *come on*," Wilhelmina squawked flapping her arms at the universe. "Give me a fucking break!"

She felt the back of her nightie strain, and, pulling it up, her eyes rotated to see behind.

"My *wings*. I got my *wings*," she sang, delighted.

"They're *tiny*," Dain said.

"Not as tiny as your *dick*!"

It was just as Alexa said. Rubbing the posterior orifices of their cloaca together was how ravens mated, but any pleasure was over in seconds. It was important to at least try while they were still partly human, but the curse remained. Sitting in silence, waiting for dawn, both slowly transformed, the chorus at first light louder than normal.

"I guess we better open the window," Wilhelmina squawked just as John Harrison's BB gun cracked the air.

"That's *it*!" she said pulling the window up, and, as if she'd always had the ability to fly, soared over to his window, grabbed the rifle, and turned it on him.

"If you ever use this on my peeps again, motherfucker, I'll blow your ugly fucking face into a million pieces and peck it to *shit*."

John, terrified, retreated inside drawing the drapes.

"*Wow*. You the GOAT!" Dain said, flying up beside her, the most magnificent mutant birdman ever.

"I guess we should follow them," Wilhelmina said indicating the flock flying into the breaking dawn.

"Dope."

****21 days later****

Wilhelmina laid three eggs after which, surprisingly, her body immediately transformed back into its human state, along with countless others in the conspiracy. People fell out of trees, off telegraph wires and roofs and the unlucky ones, straight out of the sky. The curse, finally broken.

"*Willy*? Wow, you so *Gucci*," Dain said finding her crumpled and naked at the bottom of the tree he'd left her to build a nest in alone despite it was the male raven's role during the gestation period to feed and care for her.

But no, he had flown off to rub cloaca with any old dirty bird he pleased... and not just ravens either; she had seen him get it on with a seagull, a sparrow and a budgie obviously escaped its cage before a hawk swooped down and ripped it to pieces.

She stared intently. He was Dain, but not quite Dain. He was a faded version of Dain.

With both skulking naked back to her suite, buzzing an irate Mrs. Biggar to ask her to leave her spare key in her lock, Wilhelmina could not believe what her bathroom mirror reflected–and neither could Dain; beside himself for having lost his good looks as well generous portions of his height, hair, and penis. She, tall and gorgeous, he, an ugly troll better suited to living under the bridge where he met with so many slutty pigeon girlfriends.

"You know...like...Alexa said that Ravens mate for *life*," Dain ventured, his arms reaching up to embrace her, his tiny arousal barely evident as it rubbed against the top of her knees.

"*Ye-ah... no... about* that," she said pushing him off for Snort to promptly claw his leg. "You deserted me, Dain. And while normally I really would not give a shit about looks...*you* ugly...I mean...like...*really* fucking ugly."

Dain stood stunned. Never had anyone spoken such words to him in the entirety of his life. He was Dain. *Everybody* loved Dain.

"But...but...you've *always* had a thing for me...I'm *still* Dain... Come on Willy...I mean Wilhel...."

"Just keeping it *one hundred*, dude. Now get the *fuck* out of my apartment," she said throwing his now oversized clothes at his feet.

Watching Dain slouch down the street, tripping over his too long jeans, she placed the eggs she had made him climb up her tree to retrieve on the windowsill above the baseboard heater. If legend held true, they would see the 'regurgitation' of Macha, Anad and Badb.

"Mrs. Biggar's really gonna love that!" Wilhelmina cackled to Snort who, was willing to forego the bathroom sink to rest atop the eggs instead.

"Real life witches or not, *finally*, I'll have a family. I can't wait to introduce them to Sister Pauline," she cackled maniacally just as there was an urgent banging at the door before it promptly opened, and Mrs. Biggar stood looking completely perplexed.

*"Wilhelmina...Oh...*you're not Wilhelmina...where the bloody hell is she?"

I'm *um*...her twin sister... *Willow,"* Wilhelmina said thinking on her feet. "Wilhelmina's gone for good. I'm taking over her apartment."

"Bloody hell... *Willy* and *Willow... really*? But... talk about chalk and cheese... Anyway...I was on my way to work and found this...*naked*...fool lurking in the foyer with ne'er a flyer even to cover his bloody modesty. He says he's her...*your* father...*whatever."*

Stunned, Wilhelmina could only nod.

"Honestly, your weirdo family really need to get a grip," Mrs. Biggar snapped, pushing the man in, and slamming the door.

"*Daddy*?" Wilhelmina said.

ALONE ON HALLOWEEN

By Michael Gore

The jack-o'-lantern had started to rot prematurely. Nick rolled it onto its side with the edge of his dirty sneaker; a slow-motion squishing sound softly emanated from the jagged mouth of the sad pumpkin. He shook his head with slight shame, but also as if inspecting it in the same way a detective in of those cop shows did when they hunched over a dead body.

"People always carve them too early," Nick said out loud to no one but himself, again taking up the role of a detective, his hands in his hoodie pockets.

"Day before, day before Halloween, you want them fresh." This line was mumbled more than spoken out loud. With more slight movement of his shoe, he applied pressure to the triangle-shaped eye and mashed the face into a pile of orange mush. The fact that he did it gently somehow made it alright that he had just ruined some child's pumpkin. It was on the curb of the street though, so he rationalized with himself that it was probably being thrown out anyway.

Shaking the pulpy mess off his shoe, Nick kept on his walk. It was warm—warmer than most Cabbage Nights. Nick thought of the name "Cabbage Night." Back in his hometown, the that is what they called the night before Halloween. His new town didn't have a name for it; no one even seemed to know the traditions that took place on what Nick used to think was the most fun night of the year. What he did last year on Cabbage Night, well, that was why he was in a new town—one that didn't have such traditions. His mother thought, maybe it would be "good for him" to get away and have a fresh start. After all, everything that happened last year – the destruction, the uproar in the town, and the eventual ban of trick-or-treating that next night – was one hundred percent his fault. He would never be treated fairly there again. He would always be the "kid who ruined Halloween."

Leaves crunching under his feet, some of them sticking to the drying orange muck, he thought about how long ago that year felt. It felt like another lifetime. Hell, the six months he had been living in the middle of nowhere already felt like six years. And it wasn't just time and distance. He felt like a different person now. Looking back over the past year, thinking of that awful night that was supposed to be "fun as hell," he couldn't believe how stupid he'd been. Thankfully, no one in *this* town knew him as "oh, that kid" when people mentioned his name. Now he was just the "new kid who didn't talk much." While he had no problems meeting new people and making friends, in this new town, he didn't see the point. Nick was seventeen and a senior; making friends for half a year before they all went off to college seemed pointless. Besides, most of them had been together since preschool and had bonds he couldn't even imagine. Keeping his head down and grades up was the motto: get through the year, graduate, and start a new life in college.

That's why the walk tonight seemed so...lonely. Last year, while traumatic, he was surrounded by six friends *he* had known since preschool. Friends he could trust with his life, or so he thought, until the night they all pointed their fingers right at him when the handcuffs came out. Part of him realized that is why he didn't even want friends this year: if old ones would turn on him in a second, what would new ones do? The walk, which he had already taken about a hundred times since moving into the new house, was simple and peaceful, but it had a singular purpose: snacks. While the ultimate goal was to get to the 7-Eleven for an energy drink and a few Slim Jims, Nick found himself using it as an excuse to get out of the house and enjoy the street. He already had his license, but his mother said he could not have a car until he turned eighteen and showed enough responsibility. Thankfully that was only a few months away. Regardless, Nick thought he would still take the walk. While he didn't believe in hippie crap, there was some sort of

Zen to the fourteen minutes to and fourteen minutes back that put him at ease, especially in the fall weather with the crunchy leaves making satisfying sounds under his feet—though he would never admit that to anyone and defend to his death that the walk was solely for the Slim Jims.

After two lefts, a right, and then a long straight stretch, Nick arrived at the dingy old convenience store and walked through the automatic doors. A cold burst of air hit him; they still had the air conditioning on for some reason, causing the store to be ten degrees colder than outside. The sudden cold made him hesitate with confusion for a second, but he quickly righted himself and headed for the cooler where they kept the thirty-two-ounce, overly-caffeinated drink he had become so addicted to. Opening the cooler, he paid no attention to the pumpkin decals that adorned the glass; they had already been there for a month. What he did notice was that the inside of the cooler was warmer than the store. He shook his head in frustration, but grabbed two blue cans anyway.

Three steps before the cash register, he grabbed two Slim Jims – the Monster-sized ones – and a Twix. Throwing all his stuff on the counter, he pulled the crumpled money out of his pocket. He had the exact change ready, tax included, and put it on the counter to await his cheap plastic bag. The indistinguishably foreign man behind the counter just nodded and accepted the money without looking. He knew Nick and knew his routine and the fact that he always gave the exact amount. As he cracked open a can and walked towards the door, he looked up and saw a bright orange flyer with little ghost making up a border. Nick stopped, took a sip of the acidic sludge, and read it.

Alone on Halloween?
Don't be a Ghoul
Come Out, You Fool.
Get the Scare of Your Life
Even if You're Old Enough to Have a Wife
Treats for All
Even if You Don't Survive the Fall

345 Wentworth Ave – Starts at Dusk

Make Sure to Vote for Ruben's House for
"Scariest House" this year!

It was a cheesy poster, but something about it intrigued Nick. He pulled out his phone and took a photo of the flyer and then started his walk home. The entire way he tried not to think about last year's events. Seeing the Halloween decorations, the flyer, and the countless pumpkins lining the way made him go over what happened again and again—not like he hadn't already a million times over the past year. He knew the anniversary would be hard, but he hoped that a new town would help ease the memories. It didn't.

When Nick got home, he knew he had just missed his mother because there were pumpkins on the steps that weren't there before and her car was not in the driveway. He looked at the three round, squat, but almost perfect pumpkins with no emotion, then went inside to read her note. She *always* left a note rather than just texting; she said it was *more personal*. Inside, on the fridge like always, was the large, hot pink sticky. He read it quickly; it was the same old story: she had to rush off to second job, there were frozen dinners in freezer or pizza money in drawer, don't go to bed to late, clean up, blah, blah. The only difference in this note was that she asked him to carve the pumpkins for her. *All three please, different faces on each.* It was the last thing he wanted to do, but since last year, there wasn't a single thing he didn't do that she asked. He'd been the perfect son...since November 1st of last year.

One by one he brought in the pumpkins, cleaned them off with wet paper towels, then set them down on spread out newspaper. On the television in the kitchen, he popped on AMC to watch their horror movie lineup. Thankfully, Kane Hodder was on the screen wearing the classic hockey mask and gutting people left and right. Those movies always made him happy. Nick always loved Halloween; love was probably an understatement. And yet, last year, he didn't even see a minute of his favorite holiday: he was in jail, then the courthouse, while the little kids of Bethwick cried about not being allowed to go trick-or-treating. That day, Nick knew what it felt like to be a monster—not one with latex rubber and a mask, but a real, live monster.

Pulling out the flimsy, orange, saw-like device that came with the pumpkin carving kit, Nick looked at it and sighed. The thing was three inches long and could be bent by a strong wind, yet it did a hell of a job carving through the orange flesh. Holding the tiny blade to the pumpkin to start carving an eye, Nick suddenly stopped, pulled away the saw, and slid the miniature teeth across his left wrist. It stung and left a red line, but only one tiny droplet of blood, not even enough for a sugar test, oozed out of his skin. He stared at it, then dropped the saw on the counter. He had never done anything like that in his life and it scared him. His doctors asked him countless times if he was depressed, if he ever harmed himself, if he had suicidal thoughts, and he honestly told them *no* every time. *So, what the hell was that, Nick?*

Staring blankly at the screen, seeing the giant machete in the killer's hand, Nick was suddenly happy that he did not attempt to cut the pumpkin with a real knife. With a big breath, he gently cleaned his wrist, decided it did not need a bandage, and then started to carve the pumpkins again. Watching the killer hack away on the screen, he thought of his friends back home and wondered what they were doing this night. Were they ignoring the day, refusing to relive what happened, or were they all together watching the exact same movie right now? The last three years in a row they always got together after school and raced back to one of their houses to watch the horror movie marathons and eat junk food. *Man, he missed them... God, he hated them.*

By the time the last pumpkin was done, he pushed the thoughts of his friends out of his head and the incident with the flimsy blade seemed to be a fluke that was already in the past. Looking at the pumpkins, he was proud of himself; they were not bad at all. They were not going to win any contests, but they were classic looking. After putting them outside, hoping there would be no Cabbage Night vandals like himself, he went back in and rinsed all the pumpkin seeds he set aside. His mother didn't ask him to, but he knew she loved roasted seeds, so he washed them all off, spread them on a sheet pan, covered them in oil and sea salt, and set them in the oven to cook. *Nick, making homemade snack for his hardworking mother— son of the year!*

Twenty minutes later, after one flip of the seeds, they were done. Using oven mitts, he grabbed the big cookie sheet with both hands and turned towards the counter where he had a trivet waiting, but just before he could set it down, both of his arms involuntarily pulled the tray against his chest. The red-hot lip of the pan hit his shirt with a searing popping sound, followed by a smell of burning. The heat almost instantly burnt its way through the shirt and charred his flesh. This was no quick "tap the skin, scream, and throw the pan" like a normal person would. The lip of the pan stuck deep and hard into his ribs for a solid ten seconds, until the pan itself started to adhere to Nick's melting skin. Even after he realized what he was doing, Nick never dropped the pan, nor did he scream. He simply set it on the counter, took off his gloves, and shut the oven door.

Once the off button was pushed on the oven, his screams began. Peeling off his shirt, he raced into the bathroom to see a long, fifteen-inch red, black, and brown thick line across his chest. It bubbled in parts, other parts oozed, and a few tufts of burnt gray t-shirt material stuck to his skin. Turning on the water, he quickly tried to splash his chest, but it was too late to do anything. Jumping in the shower, he turned the water to ice cold, stood under the spray, and screamed and screamed until he cried, partially from the pain, but also from not knowing what the hell just happened.

An hour later, with taped-together ice packs laid across his chest, he knew the burns needed medical attention, but he could not and would not put his mother through any sort of traumatic incident – not again, especially on the anniversary – so he was going to have to live with it for a while. Antibacterial ointment and bandages were going to have to do. If he went to the hospital, they would call her out of work. For a second year in a row, she would get a call from an official asking if Nick was her son and then telling her some horrible news. There was no way in hell he was going to do that to her again. He could live with this; it would heal eventually...he hoped.

With bandages and a new t-shirt uncomfortably on, Nick went to the kitchen to bag up the seeds. The pan itself was going to have to be thrown away. Nick just couldn't stomach trying to scrape off his own flesh to salvage the ten-dollar cookie sheet. With some painful effort, he concealed it at the bottom of the recycling bin along with the burnt t-shirt. With everything done, he skipped dinner and went to bed just as the sun started to dip down behind the horizon, the same time he put on his mask last year.

Lying in bed, Nick felt uneasy in a way he never had before. Part of him felt like he was losing his mind while part of him just didn't know what the hell was happening. The rational part was trying to tell himself that his mind was just processing last year's events in some messed up way, subconsciously punishing himself. Hell, he got off with only community service (due to his young age, a lawyer that was so expensive his mother went broke, and Nick's having no past record) even though two people...died. Maybe the guilt he thought he handled was really suppressed like his countless court-ordered therapists suggested. After endlessly talking to himself in his head, that was his best hypothesis: the date was bringing up suppressed guilt and he was subconsciously punishing himself. All he had to do was go to sleep. Tomorrow, the date will have passed, and he could start over. Nick also tried to trick his brain by telling it that he would now have a permanent, massive scar on his chest forever, which would recognize and pay tribute to his sins. He didn't think it would work, but he'd try anything to get to sleep. Which only came after four Tylenol PM.

This is a dream. Nick absolutely knew he was in a dream. Pumpkins could not talk, they could not get up and walk, they did not have legs, and they could not chase you—which meant he was dreaming. Knowing you are in a dream and waking up are two different things. When you are deep in the dream and it is still happening, when you are still running from the giant jack-o'-lantern monsters chasing you, your heart slamming, it didn't matter if you knew it was still a dream. Because it was *still* scary; it *still* felt real. As he ran for his life, he saw all the houses from the street last year, the street he had picked for a reason, the street that everything happened on. Of course, the dream would be there; of course, the nightmare would take place on that street. If this was real life, he could run through any backyard, hop a fence, and be out of that awful street. But this was a dream; there was no way out. There were walls between each house a mile high with spikes on them; he could only run from locked door to locked door while screaming for help that didn't come.

At the end of the cul-de-sac, at *the* house, Nick was out of running room; he was out of doors to try and open and windows to bang on. No one was coming to help him. *Why would they?* Turning around, he saw that there were more pumpkin monsters than he thought—there were six of them. Each with horrific grinning jack-o'-lantern faces that looked to have been carved by a madman. Inside of each raged a burning hot fire, not just a candle; flames and sparks flitted and popped out of them as they looked at him with hunger. While the faces would probably haunt his nightmares forever, it was the twisted vine bodies and legs that looked truly horrific. Spiky, slithering veins of vine made up every inch of their bodies, only when Nick looked closer, he saw they were not vines at all, but thousands of snakes writhing together.

Nick tried to speak, to plead with the monsters who were about to devour him, but his voice was gone. No words, not even a vowel, came out of his mouth. It was then that he realized his shirt was gone and the giant scar he had gotten earlier that day was on his chest, glowing bright orange, as if the line of burnt flesh was made out of molded lava. Seeing this, Nick started to cry. He wanted to fall to the ground, to run, to just give up, but he couldn't move, just like he couldn't speak. The head pumpkin monster, the tallest one, took two steps forward, fire sparking out his eyes, and pointed one writhing snake finger at Nick. Then all the other monsters followed suit and pointed their reptilian fingers at Nick. Seconds later, the lava on his chest burned so intensely he thought he was going to explode, and, in a way, he did: the burn on his skin split wide open, revealing an orange light shooting out of his chest, blinding him. The last thing he saw was all the pumpkin monsters rushing towards him.

Nick woke screaming, the wound on his chest throbbing, sweat pouring down his face. As he went to wipe his face, he screamed. His left hand was covered in orange pumpkin guts. Frantically, he shook it, flinging the stringy intestines throughout his room. Jumping up, he looked around to see if one of the monsters was actually there. Nothing. No pumpkins either. Cleaning his hand off on his comforter, Nick paced the room, wondering if he was still dreaming, but this time he understood he was not.

It took a full ten minutes of slow Box breathing to regain his composure and to think rationally. Even though he knew it was a dream and exactly what his mind was punishing him for, the pumpkin sludge was real. *Sleepwalking.* That was it—he had to have walked in his sleep and stuck his hands in one of the jack-o'-lanterns. *Right?* Regardless what happened, he was scared and he felt awful; his body was sore from tensing, the burn was unbearable, and he was miserable. After gaining some of his composure, he dared look at the result of last night's self-mutilation. Puss had oozed through the bandages and dried, sealing his shirt to his skin with a layer of crunchy browns, blacks, and reds. It took almost half an hour to pull the shirt and bandages off, and when he did, it just reopened the wound. The sight of the injury made him nauseous and also reconfirmed that he should have gone to the hospital...and probably still should. Hell, if his mind continued the way it was, he would end up in the hospital for sure.

After an excruciatingly painful shower, more ointment, bandages and a fresh shirt, Nick went into the kitchen to find a bowl next to a box of cereal and another pink sticky note. He wasn't surprised to read that his mom had to leave early, again, to go to her first job of the day. It also went on with almost the exact same wording as the day before and the day before that: *Sorry I missed you. Have a great day at school, honey. Let's catch up this weekend.* The only thing that differed this time was one line asking him to hand out candy tonight, and when he ran out, to shut the lights off. Nick hated that buying more than two small bags of candy was now a luxury his mother couldn't afford. Yet again, he was ruining some kid's Halloween, even if it was by just getting one less piece of candy.

Snapping on the television, he poured himself some berry-flavored, Frankensteinthemed cereal and enjoyed the irony of eating it on the one day of the year the cereal was relevant. On the screen before him, he watched as morning show hosts jumped around in asinine costumes that weren't meant to scare, but instead get an *aww* from the crowd. Nick shook his hand with slight anger, but he pushed it away. It was that anger and thought that had started the whole situation last year. A simple conversation about the origins of Halloween and why it was *supposed* to be scary. *Not cute, not silly, not sexy...scary.* Dressing up as cute princesses and superheroes made no sense at all. Demons were supposed to come to Earth on All Hallows' Eve; if they saw terrible monsters and fellow demons, they would be satisfied that Earth was in shambles, or better yet, they would get scared and retreat back to where they came from. A sexy nurse and a superhero would not scare a demon. That rabbit hole of a conversation is what lead to his "idea" to scare the shit out his town to try and bring back the roots of Halloween. He just never thought it would work that well.

Pouring his second bowl, he suddenly found himself standing. He didn't remember even getting up nor understood why he did. Then, with the speed of a falling cinderblock, Nick slammed his head into his cereal bowl. Thankfully, with a split-second thought, he turned his head slightly so the left side of his face took the brunt force. The rim of the hard and red ceramic bowl dug into his flesh and then exploded, sending cereal, pink milk, and shards of sharp red flying in every direction. Lifting his head back up, Nick knew without a doubt that there were going to be pieces of the bowl stuck in his scalp and cheek. Calmly as he could, he went to the bathroom and looked in the mirror. Sure enough, there were several marshmallows, a few cute pink pieces of cereal, a whole lot of milk, and half a dozen chunks of the bowl protruding from the side of his face. He removed the cereal first and pulled out the shards one by one, the entire time acting like he was doing nothing but gently pulling lint off his face.

Twenty minutes later, after washing his face and treating the wounds, which thankfully were not deep, he had realized he had missed the bus, but he didn't care. There was no way he could go to school and risk doing something like that in front of a teacher. He'd end up in the looney bin before lunch. He had to stay home and make sure he didn't harm himself again. Things were getting way too dangerous.

Nick desperately wanted his mom, but he just couldn't do that to her: he couldn't make her leave work, and worse, he couldn't make her worry about him...not again. The trial last year had almost killed her. She was so devastated that her hair went half-gray, she started taking anxiety medication, and she saw a therapist twice a week. While she claimed she was fine on a consistent basis, he could tell she was holding everything together by a thread. Nick did not want to be the one to cut that last thread, especially since he was already the one who unraveled the others.

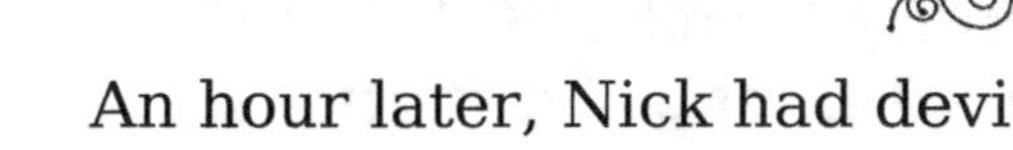

An hour later, Nick had devised a contraption to keep himself safe. It wasn't anything complicated or foolproof, but it should protect him enough from any other major impulses...at least he hoped. It involved several pillows, two oven mitts, and two old blue jump ropes he found in a storage box. With his hands in the gloves, the pillows all around him, his legs tied shut, and one hand tied to his bedpost, he figured one padded hand couldn't do much damage. Beforehand, he was smart enough to put some food and drinks next to the bed as well as the ever-important pee bottle. And that is how Nick sat for the next six hours, doing nothing but snacking and watching *Halloween 1, 2,* and *4* all in a row. Having seen the movies ten times each, if not more, it was insanely boring to not be able to play on his phone at the same time, but at least the movies made it feel like it was officially "Halloween."

When three o'clock came around, the time he would normally be home from school after the bus dropped him off and he got his normal snack at the store, he dared untying himself, as there hadn't been a single incident. Besides, he needed to stretch. To be safe, he kept the oven mitts on for the next hour as he cautiously moved around the house, as if waiting for someone to attack him. At four o'clock, when nothing still had happened and he saw the first of the very little children start to go door to door, he slipped off the gloves and put on his orange pumpkin t-shirt and got the bowl of candy ready.

Over the next two hours, he dutifully answered the door, put on a happy smile, and gave out candy while complimenting the costumes. Princess after princess, superhero after superhero, the occasional fireman or cop, and a few cartoon characters he didn't recognize came one after another. Not a single monster, goblin, troll, or serial killer in the bunch. Of course, every single mother had cat ears, drawn on whiskers, and a cheap tail, as if it were a law that once you became a mom, you had to wear the cat paraphernalia. It depressed Nick, but he was happy not to have harmed himself, especially in front of a child. Mostly, he was just happy he was getting to have somewhat of a Halloween this year.

As the last candy was handed out, well before seven o'clock when the older, more demanding kids would start coming, Nick sighed and shut off all the outdoor lights and most of the indoor ones. Sitting in his room, with just the television on, hearing the laughter from the hordes outside, Nick felt a deep depression wash over him. Guilt, self-loathing, anger, and the events of last year started to bounce around his head like sharp daggers, each one sticking in and causing a ripple of pain that wouldn't leave. Thankfully it was only mental pain, as he truly didn't think he could handle any more physical pain on top of his burn. Even the horror marathon on the television couldn't stop his mind; it was so fast and brutal, he wasn't even sure what movie was playing. As he tried to focus to see what masked killer was on the television, the desire to hurt himself crept into his brain. This scared him, as during the other times he'd felt nothing before they happened. This time, he knew something *was* going to happen. Jumping out of bed, he took deep breaths and paced back and forth. Air was not getting into his lungs enough; he simply couldn't get a solid breath. It was as if the air in the house was not clean enough. *He needed air. Fresh air.*

Less than twenty second later, Nick was outside sucking in glorious, clean autumn air. On the street there was dozens of kids. They all looked so damn happy, their parents laughing and smiling as they held their bags and went door to door. Nick missed his Mom and he missed being a kid. It was so much easier then. The thought of going back in the house made him sick. Being outside with the fresh air and the happiness of the children made him feel...sane. So, he decided to take his normal walk towards the store. He didn't even know if he wanted to go to the store or where he was going, but it seemed to be the most natural path to follow. Normally the street was so lonely and peaceful he could walk it blindfolded and not bump into a thing or another person. Tonight, there were so many children and adults walking in every direction he had to zig and zag constantly...and it made him happy. Here in this town, Halloween was still a happy event and he was nearly invisible. No one was looking at him with disgust and anger; everyone he brushed past smiled or nodded, and some even told him, "Happy Halloween." The air and looking at costumes were helping him calm and keep his mind off of everything. Slowing his pace, he started to relax and take in the beauty of the holiday. It was magical. It truly was the only day of the year you would see so many people out on the streets after dark. And while Nick still thought it was a night that was meant to scare away the demons trying to creep into our earth, he couldn't help but love what it had become after hearing the laughter and excitement of all the children.

Leisurely strolling, watching the kids and teens run from house to house, he simply people-watched and enjoyed the seasonally warm air. Slowly but surely, his mind settled and he was enjoying the night. As a few teens walked by, he heard them talk about the "the kick-ass haunted house." It was then that he recalled the flyer he saw in the store the other day. Pulling out his phone, he opened his photos and found the shot he took, noted the street, and pulled up his map; it was only a seven-minute walk. As he headed directly there, he realized this town *was* pretty cool. His old town didn't have all sorts of contests for "Best Halloween Decorations" and "Scariest House." Hell, his old town was so stuffy, the city board once made a family remove a hanging skeleton from their yard, stating that it was "too disturbing" for locals. This town was *supporting* Halloween. *If I'd lived here my whole life, I wouldn't have pushed back so hard, those people wouldn't have died, and I wouldn't have...whatever the hell I have right now,* Nick thought to himself with a pang of sorrow.

As he walked, each street got more and more festive. Almost every house was fully decorated, there were entire displays in front yards, people hanging out and partying, music playing, laughing everywhere. It was heaven. Turning down Wentworth Avenue, Nick was shocked to see it was even crazier than the last few streets he walked down. Instead of *almost*, *every* single house on the street was lit up with purple and orange lights, some lawns had bubbling cauldrons, others had intricate setups with flying bats and spiders on strings that would swoop down and scare trick-or-treaters. Not a single home had the lights off. Almost every resident was sitting outside in lawn chairs, some by fires, having a hell of a time handing out candy to every person. Nick even noticed that most of the houses had *cases* of candy to ensure they did not run out, not two bags. And it wasn't the cheap stuff either; they weren't handing out dollar store candy because of the volume. These people were handing out the real stuff. Some houses even gave out full-size bars. As he walked, looking at the house numbers, Nick realized he was smiling; it was probably the most real smile he had in a year.

As he came up to one particular house, he noticed a cave-like entrance with smoke coming out of it and a line of teenagers and adults waiting to get in, moving around with giddy anticipation. Nick was always more on the shy side and didn't really like to do things alone, which is why the last year had been so hard with his not having friends anymore, but without thinking, he joined the line. It wasn't the house number on the flyer, but he might as well see the other houses to judge if the other house truly was the best. Seconds later, there were a dozen more people behind him. Everyone was talking, laughing, and acting nervous, especially the girls holding onto the guys. Seeing that gave him a pang in his heart so strong it made him touch his chest, which reminded him of his burn. His pointer finger lightly touching his shirt felt like a bullet hitting his chest. He let out an audible gasp and hunched over, sucked air, and tried not to cry. As he whimpered, he could hear whispers behind him, so he pretended to pick a piece of something up off the ground and put the imaginary thing in his pocket, his chest still stinging.

Entering the mouth of the cave, his visibility was cut down to almost nothing. The dense fog and strobing lights made it hard to see, but he edged his way forward, trying to keep an eye on the shoulder of the teen boy wearing the Jason mask in front of him. It was a bit disorienting, but that was good: you shouldn't feel safe in a haunted house. A few seconds later, he was suddenly in what was clearly a garage, though there were black tarps up and giant pots with bubbling green liquid and two poorly dressed witches laughing ridiculous laughs and cackling at the passersby. It was pretty cheesy, but Nick gave them a nod and a smile to show he approved of the effort these homeowners did. Just as he did, the witch pointed at Nick and screamed his name.

"Nick, Nick, that boy was sure sick, sick." No one knew his name in this town. Hearing it caused him to stop in his tracks and the line of people behind him bumped into him. He stared at the witch, who didn't look away from him, her fake nose held on with string…yet he was getting scared of her. As the group started to push him along, he saw the woman reach into the pot and pull out a human head. The second he saw the graying hair, he knew who it would be: it was Mr. D's head, his teacher...who died last year. Nick screamed and ran like he was in a bad horror movie, pushing patrons out of the way, getting dirty looks and called names, but he didn't care. He had to get out of the house. The line was clogged at the entrance to the basement – *damn, these people used their entire house* – so he pushed his way through a black tarp, ripping it off the wall and burst out the front door of the house. Someone ran out after him screaming, but they gave up when he got off the yard.

Running was making his chest feel like Freddy Krueger was giving him a massage, so he slowed his pace and once again did some Box breathing. *It was your imagination, nothing more. The woman didn't call your name and the head she pulled out was fake. Calm the hell down.* Sitting on the curb, he leaned against the tree and watched the wonderful world of Halloween walk by, slowly calming with each breath. Part of him wanted to go home, but the other part of his brain gave him a pep talk telling him it was safer to be out with people. At least if he had a breakdown here, someone would call for help, and if he tried to hurt himself, some heroic soccer mom or dad would jump in and save him. Besides, even with his brain falling apart, he was still having the best night he had in years. Besides, he still hadn't seen the best haunted house. Nick decided to stay out and keep walking around until the pumpkins started to get blown out.

After walking a bit more, taking in some displays that would rival real haunted houses and theme parks, Nick finally came upon number three-forty-five. Just like the other houses, there was a line of teens and adults alike waiting to go through the homemade haunted house. Nick was hesitant after the last one, but joined the back of the line, ready for whatever lay ahead. This time, if something bizarre happened, he was going to ignore it and fight back against his brain. He wouldn't let his mind win. This was his Halloween and he was going to enjoy, even if it killed him.

Looking ahead to the front of the line, he noticed a little green light flicker on that told the next group when to walk through the black tarp tunnel that went along the side of the house to the backyard. All the houses seemed to have a tunnel like this, but it made sense. They all needed an entrance after all. Thinking about just building one of these tunnels and setting up a light-based entrance system, Nick couldn't believe the amount of work put into something that was free and just for locals. It made him happy that there were others out there like him that truly loved and believed in the holiday. And while he wouldn't admit it out loud, he hoped one day he could turn his own house into a haunted one every year.

In front of him, he noticed a group of three teens. He recognized them from school but he didn't know their names. One girl was clearly with her boyfriend, as they couldn't keep their hands off each other, but the third was alone and seemed awkward being the third wheel. Nick tried not to pay attention to her, but she kept looking back and smiling at him. After three groups walked through the tunnel, she turned and talked to him.

"You're that new kid, right?" Nick smiled and nodded; he quickly stuck his hand out and told her his name. When he heard her name was Laurie, Nick laughed out loud, which got a strange reaction from her.

"Your name is the same as the main character in the *Halloween* movies. I can't believe I'm meeting a Laurie *on* Halloween." The girl laughed shyly and said her mom actually named her after the character because she wanted her child to be a "survivor." Nick's heart skipped a beat hearing this. As the line moved forward, Nick was introduced to the other two kids who didn't seem to care much about meeting him, but that was fine—he didn't care about them either. As the line slowly moved, he talked and talked to Laurie, who eventually asked if he would go through the house *with* her. He agreed without hesitation, thrilled he hadn't given up and gone home. The smile she gave back to him melted everything away and made him realize things would be alright in life.

A few moments later, it was their turn to walk inside. Laurie got close to Nick and he felt his heart race. For the first time that night, the pain of the burn was tolerable. The tunnel was darker than he thought it would be and he actually got a bit creeped out. Unlike the other house, this one had a creepy ambient noise and a laser making a vortex-looking image at the end of the tunnel. The first few jump scares were mostly animatronic spiders and monsters bought at the seasonal Halloween shop. They were effective, but not terrifying by any means. The best part about them: they made Laurie jump and grab Nick's arm. The light touch of her hands on his arm radiated through his entire body. The touch was so subtle, but to Nick and his deflated heart, it felt like a giant fireworks display was being set off inside of him.

The tunnel curved around the back of the house; the other couple was a good ten feet in front of them. Nick could see there was a big scare at the turn as the two jumped, screamed, and scurried away. Knowing something big coming up made Laurie grab tight to Nick's arm, preparing for the jolt. A giant scarecrow jumped out from behind a black tarp, almost making contact with Nick's face. The noise and movement were so sudden, Laurie jumped away, losing the grip on Nick and running towards her friends, who were laughing and standing at the end of the tunnel. Nick, on the other hand, didn't move, for the face he saw staring back from the scarecrow was his own—not *really* his own, but he saw himself behind the rubbery, toothy grin of the macabre scarecrow. It was the exact same mask *he* had worn last Cabbage Night. Suddenly, all the warm fuzzy fun he was having drained from his body. There were all sorts of noises around him – yelling, screaming, laughing, haunted music, and canned cackles – but all Nick could hear was the sickening rip of flesh he heard last year. As the scarecrow slowly moved away from his face and reset, Nick shook his head and tried to tell himself it was just a coincidence this time and not his mind slipping yet again. Nick wanted the warm firework feeling of Laurie's hands on him again; he could fight the past and have a new life in this town, maybe with Laurie. Turning to find her, he saw the door at the end of the long black hall shut; her friends must have pulled her with them.

Racing to the door, he saw a red light on telling him to *Wait...or Else*. He ignored it and tried the door, but it didn't open. Hearing the piston hiss behind him, sending the scarecrow launching at the next group, he couldn't stop himself; he shouldered the door and burst into the room. It was obviously another garage, but the owner had done a hell of a job setting it up to look like some sort of Satanic ritual. There was a man dressed as a cult leader in a red robe standing in front of a rubbery dead body laying across an altar, but Laurie was already gone. Nick let out a small laugh—not because he thought it was stupid, but because he was happy and excited about how cool the room looked. This was not some cheesy witch—this was *dark*. If he had more time, he would have loved to take in the room, but he couldn't lose Laurie, so he started to jog across the room towards the exit. Something caught his foot, which he only saw a glimpse of, but it looked to be a giant hand made of...pumpkin vines. Being that he was jogging, the sudden stopping of his foot sent him flying, face-first, into the hard concrete.

As his nose shattered, Nick saw a brilliant flash of light. When his two front teeth tore through his upper lip, he saw darkness. In the darkness, he saw the face of his old teacher and the girl who died last year. They were playing together, happy and content in the fall leaves. The image made Nick happy. He tried to smile, but his teeth protruding through his lip would not allow any sort of facial expressions to be made. In a hazy state, he felt hands on his body rolling him over. He tried to open his eyes, but the pain and blood pooling around them did not allow that either. All he could do was gurgle.

There was a bright light shone in his eyes; he could see the brightness through his bruising lids and he heard an adult talking to him, but he could still see the man and the girl playing and he didn't want to let go of that image. Then the hands were off of him and he was alone again. In his vision he saw the little girl jump into the leaves and disappear, but when she jumped out of them, she was bloody and her face torn, just like his was now. The image shocked him back into consciousness. Opening his eyes just a tiny sliver, he saw a man – the man he saw when he entered the room – dressed in a cult leader's robe, fixing the door he had just broke. Two seconds later, the man was picking him up. Nick thought of Laurie and wondered if she was waiting outside and if she would ever talk to him again with a broken nose and split lip.

Then, the man placed him, with a lot of pulling and struggling, onto the altar. This confused Nick, as he didn't know why the man wouldn't have just let him lay there until the ambulance came. The table was uncomfortable and his head dangled backwards, sending blood dripping down his throat. He tried to speak again, but there was too much blood choking him.

"The judges are coming through next...Sorry, kid, but I'm not losing to my brother again this year." Through blurry eyes, Nick could see a hidden monitor on the floor by the man's feet: three people with clipboards were coming down the tunnel. Nick then watched the man pick up a very realistic looking knife, and then he heard the buzz of the door. The man started to speak loudly, some Latin-sounding chant, and raised the knife high above Nick.

In the moment before the blade came down, Nick realized that everything in the past year was leading up to this. That no matter how good he was, no matter what he did, it was his destiny to die. They were never going to let him live; he needed to be punished for what he had done. They just wanted him to suffer for a year before finally taking his life from him. Now, just like his horrible tricks turned wrong, he was about to meet his demise at the hands of another person taking Halloween just a bit *too* far. His vision getting cloudier, he looked to the man; the pumpkin monsters were standing over his shoulder, looking down at him with large laughing grins.

As the knife plunged into his chest, slicing through his burns, he heard the gasps from the judges and one person say, "That is so realistic!"

With his last breath, Nick whispered, "I'm sorry," but then he tried to smile, because he knew that his death would become the stuff of legends and a tale that kids would tell each other forever as they avoided this house every Halloween.

DANCE OF MASKS AND FIRE
THE WITCHFINDER'S SHADOW

By Greg Patrick

"I am no more a witch than you are a wizard, and if you take away my life, God will give you blood to drink."
~Sarah Good, one of the 20 people executed during the Salem Witchcraft Trials.

───────────────

"Shall we never never get rid of this Past? ... It lies upon the Present like a giant's dead body."
~Nathaniel Hawthorne, *The House of the Seven Gables*

———————— ❧

Salem, Massachusetts
21st century

I

Revenant

The rare apparition of an Al Hallows Eve moon cast its spell of eerie pallor and spotlight across the cobbled streets, illuminating ornaments of skeletons swaying from branches like a hangman's Christmas tree. Lighting them in passing with an apparitional caress and lingering on the old gabled colonial house, bathing its resplendently. Within its aging vined walls its tenant thrashed in the throes of nightmare-haunted sleep, tormented by recurring nightmares. In the days leading to All Hallows eve they were becoming more vivid. Then the house was cast in sudden ominous darkness...like a murder of crows drawn to scavenge a terrible battle there was a sudden gathering of darkness...a cauldrenous massing of rapidly shifting storm clouds glowered over the town, growling with thunder like the belly of a grim dark god hungering for offerings.

He awoke with a cry...disoriented....
wondered where he was....as much as when he
was. In the rising wind that sounded like a
disembodied cry, the leafless branches scraped
the window like skeletal hands clawing for him.
He arose and like a somnambulist and
approached the great mullioned window
overlooking the street. Its panes were lit in
intervals by lightning...A disembodied song
seemed to haunt the air enticing him like a dark
carol's serenade of venomed honey.

He peered outside, and she was there,
illuminated for a jolting moment in an eerie
spectral glow of lightning, standing against a
background of jack o lanterns. Her pale
expressionless face looking up at him
expectantly...in a dark frilled gown and
porcelain harlequin mask...she seemed to blow
a sarcastic kiss at him then seemingly
dematerialised in an interval of darkness.

The mime.

The mysterious stranger who had been his
second shadow since the leaves turned flame
red...At first her sudden intrusions had been
mildly amusing, then annoying, then somehow
concerning...

He had first seen her pale masked dance into his path on his walk back home...the usual routine of palms feeling at an invisible barrier between them. He had quickened his pace, shrugging her off dismissively...yet her appearances were unpredictable but numerous and calculated. She began reappearing jarringly from the leaf-strewn alleyways...then she would disappear as suddenly. He clutched the windowsill meeting her dark eyes...Then an interval of darkness and she had vanished...yet again...

Veiled by darkness, she lingered unseen, as he retreated from the window. She stood in cold rapture as the rain fell like pent-up tears hailing her...Her arms spread, like the conductor of a danse macabre...rallying the ancestral ghosts of Salem...Her rage and power were a force of nature like the raging storm that swept her soul. War had been declared...in that historic town that oozed dark secrets as if from reopened wounds.

Who was he?

He was a guide at the historic house, for as long as any could remember. The novice docents idolised him and the local paper dubbed him a living treasure...

Morbid vultures he privately scowled of the patrons who eagerly flocked to the historic infamous town with a dark past.

Mr. Elmer, the veteran docent who made the past come alive to the tour groups, transplanted his audience to another time as he ushered them through the house, relishing the chime of steady coins in appreciative tip jars.

Who was she? The mystery lingered...haunted him...as the nights grew longer and darker....and skeletons, black cats, and witches appeared on the trees...in feverish expectation for Halloween in infamous Salem. The storm had raged through the streets like a mad poltergeist...strewn with debris. Torn Halloween decorations lay amid leaves like an explosion's aftermath.

II

Across Red Dreamscapes

"By the pricking of my thumbs, Something wicked this way comes."

~ William Shakespeare, Macbeth

"Hell is empty and all the devils are here."

~ William Shakespeare, *The Tempest*

He sank into sleep again... *writhing in the throes of nightmares that haunted his immortal's sleep like a danse macabre of ghosts amid castle ruins...*remembering a night like this...*centuries before...when he roared from the pulpit...rallying his* congregation against a coven of witches he insisted were bedevilling Salem, his oratory raised to maddened heights of righteous indignation. He suddenly pointed figures at women in the congregation...

"Behold witches in our midst!"...women who screamed as they were grabbed and dragged away...women who had foolishly rejected his lecherous advances...

He gloated inwardly...This was all too easy...None in Salem would refuse him again he was sure...Until he paid a call on one of his parishioners and tried his hand at a proud Irish midwife in their employ...Refusal???

"Witch!!!" He howled, pointing a trembling finger at her...blood oozing from between his fingers as he clutched his cheek where her nails scratched as he tried to press her down into the barn's hay.

"Popish heathen! "he had denounced her.

An Irish midwife among English puritans...She had fled his hired thugs into the night forest, under cover of mist and darkness...eluding their relentless pursuit in the labyrinthine wood...

Suddenly the witch hunter stood in the clearing in the moonlight...and raised a thrashing figure...

"Yield sorceress! I have your familiar!" Her beloved cat...

She stifled a cry...

"Come hither or I will have my men butcher the wretched demon alive..."

She stepped forward from the sanctuary of shadows and was roughly grasped...

"Now unhand him..."

He laughed gloatingly moving to snap the cat's neck, only to scream as its claws raked his face. He let it go and it disappeared into the darkness soundlessly...He presided over her execution, next to him the russet sack masked executioner at the gallows. Her face in the tear-shaped frame of a noose...A w had been branded on her cheek to mark her as a condemned witch...Her face was set and composed as a porcelain mask.

He always savoured their cries and whimpering as the noose was tightened at their throat. Yet she laughed...laughed...the ultimate heresy...

"Cry! he demanded. "Cry damn you! Whimper and plead for your life! All my victims cry," he hissed.

"Shed tears and I will mercifully hasten your demise... "he offered.

Shrilly she cursed at them in her native tongue of Irish Gaelic, her last words like a battle cry that would echo in recurring nightmares for centuries... Cursing them and theirs and him most of all.

"She is summoning her dark power!" Someone screamed...

"Silence her! Save us!"

Her teeth were forced open as he gripped her hair...A heated pronged torture instrument sizzled into her tongue.... severing it..."Now!" He ordered.

He knew the dark art of execution...none of his accused died quickly at the rope.... The trapdoor opened and she swayed kicking.... before shuddering spasmodically and swaying....

He asked a bounty hunter who he sent to track down fugitive accused witches..."You served with Cromwell...you know something of her savage tongue do you not?"

"That I do your eminence...she was cursing you..."

"Well I imagine she wasn't showering me with sonnets..."

"Ye miss my meaning.... cursing prophetically...you and Salem...for all time...something about never dying and looking for you..."

He snorted derisively...

He pulled a Celtic cross from her neck...a talisman she treasured...he always took a memento of his victims as a grisly trophy....

He looked up then over the crowd and saw her black cat perched on a tree branch watching the execution...its eyes smouldered crimson in the torchlight...it hissed baring its fangs before slipping down like a dark tear drop and melting away into the darkness...

She seemed harmless enough swaying with head covered in a sack...yet something hypnotically pendulum-like in the motions...and the visions it inspired would haunt his dreams...Never dying...

When the opinions of the prominent turned against his witch hunts he relented in his persecutions...yet his insatiable desire to inflict pain clawed at his mind till he turned to other targets...He vowed from his pulpit to bring civilisation with scripture and sword to the heathen savages who dwelled in the forest.

Like a dark lord on crusade, he led at the vanguard pikemen and musketmen, he himself astride a fine horse and clad strikingly in armoured breastplate and helm...he even permitted himself the vanity of a crimson plume for his morion helm...A brace of pistols across his chest and sabre sheathed at his side...He anticipated the butchery with a mad smile...And it was all too easy...The village was taken by fire and sword, its people fell screaming to volleys or were ran through with pikes if they fled. He felt intoxicated with the bloodletting. Those who had been spared in the onslaught were chained in a line to be force-marched back triumphantly to Salem.

As his men erupted in huzzahs, he scanned the faces of the living and slain. The infirm, the elderly, women with children...Where were the braves? His question was answered as his horse snorted blood as its flanks was riddled with arrows. It reared and collapsed under him, pinning him down.

A wild choir of ululating battle cries like a sudden maelstrom tore the air. His men hastily tried to reload and powder their muskets and perished trying as they were slashed down by vengeful braves.

"The savage is upon us! Form ranks!" He cried...

Charging under cover of a cauldrenous shroud of mist, they erupted into the clearing howling for revenge. He watched in grim detached fascination as his men went down fighting, screaming in agony as they were ritually maimed.

One man was pinned down by multiple warriors while another dissected him with a flint dagger. Shrill cries announced that initiated youths had made their first kill, raising a severed part of their assailant's body in the air as proof to their chieftain. He freed himself at last, and tried to crawl furtively away...

A warrior looked up from his slain enemy baring his teeth like a wolf over his kill. His face warpainted a ghostly pale...the blood flowing from his tomahawk strike like crimson tears down his face. He closed in on the witch hunter, who felt a foot press him down and forcibly roll him onto his back...He closed his eyes in anticipation, yet the dreaded blow never fell. Looking down on him was the Tribe's shaman, ritually wolf-masked.

"I see you recognise me as a man of stature to my people...Indeed I am.

And it is very much in your interest to allow me to depart unscathed and with humble apologies...To do otherwise would be to invite terrible reprisals on your people..."

In the tense silence he heard the screams of ritual mutilations inflicted on his wounded former militia. The Shaman was handed an array of small barbed blades...He made his choice...

He was left...alive...Death wasn't painful enough...He was mortally wounded...horribly maimed. He was left begging for death, left for the wolves to finish off and ravens to scavenge...Yet as he staggered with wolves howling in the background in eerie choir...he felt his wounds healing rapidly...

How?

The curse!

He fled the colonies...living in self-imposed exile across the sea...where he delved into the occult himself and studied the dark arts under the best warlocks and necromancers in the world...

One night he betrayed his master and killed him for the coveted sceptre of Hades...its wielder could command the dead...

"With it, I hold sway over All Hallows eve!" He had all but howled in lycanthropic rapture.

His self-imposed exile from Salem ended when he arrived at the door of the museum centuries later and auditioned as a tour guide...

The artifacts displayed there, were a witch-hunter's trophy room...He kept souvenirs of each victim like a modern serial killer...Again he felt at home.

III

Wizard's Duel

"It was written I should be loyal to the nightmare of my choice."

~Joseph Conrad, *Heart of Darkness*

And it was the afternoon of Halloween.
And all the houses shut against a cool wind.
And the town was full of cold sunlight.
But suddenly, the day was gone.
Night came out from under each tree and spread."
~Ray Bradbury, "The Halloween Tree"

"All these, however, were mere terrors of the night, phantoms of the mind that walk in darkness; and though he had seen many spectres in his time, and been more than once beset by Satan in divers shapes, in his lonely pre-ambulations, yet daylight put an end to all these evils; and he would have passed a pleasant life of it, in despite of the devil and all his works, if his path had not been crossed by a being that causes more perplexity to mortal man than ghosts, goblins, and the whole race of witches put together, and that was - a woman."

~Washington Irving, *The Legend of Sleepy Hollow*

All Hallows eve was ushered in by a moan of cold wind, sweeping through the town like a flight of ravens bearing dark tidings to all who yet understood its dark speech...tossing its bloodred leaves like red debris...scattering it in tribute before a lone figure watching from the street, whispering through her raven hair.

For his part, the old witchfinder of Salem, felt rejuvenated and invincible as he strode out. He basked in the apparitional spotlight of moonbeams. The facade of affable host shed like serpent skin.

Tonight, he would travel in style, he thought. He would hire a horse-drawn carriage with plumed horses. Yet by some trick of the light it seemed the town looked older...The way he remembered it...no cars roaring between the gabled houses, no mobs of revellers...What was afoot?

The mime he suspected.

Her hand is in this!

If it is a duel, she wanted...

He donned his powdered wig and primed his flintlock pistols...

Once again, he felt himself, the dark lord of Salem, leading hired thugs that seemed to rise in lumbering shadows, trailing him. The wind rose like conjured ghosts tearing Halloween decorations down.

"I will purge the city again of this heathen abomination..."

He cursed suddenly as a black cat undulated across his path. It paused in mid-step and hissed. It reappeared in golden-eyed Vigil in its usual haunt perched on the gabled roof, back arched in a perpetual question mark poised to the night, motionless as a dark chimera, saw him in monochrome, baring its teeth...

As he advanced along the street a solitary gowned figure watched his diminishing form, racing the darkness. Sinuously, undulantly the cat approached her, fondly nuzzling her. She gathered him up, tenderly cradling him.

How I have missed thee, she thought.

Suddenly two misshapen diminutive figures lurched towards her, detaching from a pack of trick or treaters they had mingled with. They tugged at her hems like grovelling and fawning courtiers...

"Whither does our mistress seek her quarry How may we serve thee? *"one masked like a dark jester addressed her with a tri-echo rasp.*

Its nostrils snorted at a glove the witch finder had dropped, inhaling its stench and then scenting the air for its former wearer. Like hounds in eager anticipation of their huntress's whim, they clawed the ground and whined restlessly to be unleashed.

Meanwhile, the witch hunter cursed at the sight of the memorial shrine dedicated to the man and women of Salem that had been executed in Salem for witchcraft. It was a glowing reminder that outside the oubliette walls of his historic home and narrative, the world had changed. He felt like an awkward relic...nauseated by it all...the laughter and merrymaking of a festival he had once personally outlawed, when he was the great witchfinder cleric of Salem, denouncing women from his pulpit. Any he so much as disliked perished at his word. Now he was merely relegated to a tourist attraction, a parody of his former esteemed self.

The shrine shimmered with vigil candles, constellated like a gothic birthday cake. He moved to trod down flowers left in tribute.

"Still displacing your impotent rage against us centuries later. "a voice taunted from the darkness.

"Who said that? "he demanded.

He saw her then...A solitary figure dancing gracefully, supple limbs weaving in flamenco like motions, as if in a sacred dance. Suddenly her arms lowered languidly, as if aware of his presence for the first time. She slowly pivoted to face him.

The mime....

"What do you want from me? "

She raised a finger to her porcelain lips for silence and raised a jack o lantern as if brandishing a medusa's head, gloating fire at him.

As if ventriloquised, it addressed him in a lilting brogued voice...

"Well met then witchfinder...We cross paths again...three centuries to the day...I told you I'd return for thee..."

She pulled her mask down then...a face he had not seen since a dark sack was placed over her noose-ringed head at the gallows....

He recoiled then. His sense of omnipotence deflated like a swollen plague sore lanced and drained of its putrid contents.

He raised a crucifix to hold her at bay, yet cried out in agony as the silver cross sizzled into his palm, branding his flesh and rejecting his touch. Yet there were other ways to vanquish his enemies. He drew the sceptre of Hades.

She uttered a counterspell through the jack o lantern. As incantations were delivered it seemed the shadows of two dark hounds were cast on the wall tearing at each other, though no beast was there...She raised her arms suddenly with a dark flourish.

"Rise sisters! "

A chill wind rose, extinguishing the candles and her masked face confronted him, like a pale free-floating appartional head.

"En Garde!" He pointed the sceptre at her like a rapier foil.

Suddenly a small dark figure leapt from the shadows with simian agility and tore the sceptre from his grasp, squealing and cavorting with impish merriment

"And touché!!! How now then witch finder?"

He scampered away, howling with glee. He pivoted to face her again, drawing and cocking his flintlock pistol...Yet again she had vanished. Suddenly the jack o lanterns flared up with hellish intensity and he cried out and ran in pursuit of the impish figure, waving the sceptre triumphantly as he fled. Yet the imp, moved with supernatural speed, maddeningly eluding his grasp.

He arrived at a crossroads marked by a great ancient tree...

"Where are ye devil? Nothing evil can escape me... "

"Especially not yer past. Devil am I? Hobgoblin actually!

Know yer unearthly denizens. You are about to meet them all tonight."

He sprang onto a tree and hung upside down grinning at him madly like a Cheshire cat.

"Much ado about this old stick. Want it? Here..."

He cast it to the cobbles and just as he reached for it...the goblin somersaulted from the tree, acrobatically and grabbed it up again, just in the shadow of his palm....

He lifted the flintlock and suddenly his throat was lassoed from behind by the throat. He was lifted as if being hanged from the tree branch, as his goblin cohorts perched on the tree squealed with glee.

They played panpipes as his legs kicked....

"Oh, look at him dance! And a merry reel at that! "

Suddenly the branch broke and he gasped painfully on the ground...

He rose again and with a howl of animal rage pursued the hobgoblin. The cohort of goblins cast the sceptre in relays as they scurried away with him bellowing in pursuit. Suddenly the hobgoblin paused mid-leap and ran in place cringing at some unsightly spectacle...A Santa and deer on a rooftop with lights. His eyes smouldered and he hissed...

"Where is he?" Mr. Elmer wondered aloud.

His eyes were drawn to a row of elf-hatted decorations standing triumphantly over Santa being hanged by the Christmas lights and the reindeer heads mounted like hunting trophies.

Santa's severed head was replaced by a jack o lantern-headed scarecrow on the sleigh...

They leaped from rooftop to rooftop and onto the street, leading him on....

"And what a merry chase have we!" The hobgoblin squealed.

They were approaching a crowd of people eagerly lined up for a walk through haunted house. The hobgoblin was at the threshold, his eyes smouldering with glee...

"Trick or treat!" He mocked, holding up the sceptre...

Sweeping past objections, Mr. Elmer pushed through the line and stormed into the haunted house, drawing his sabre and slashing through the cobwebs, machete-like. Eerie music was playing...Suddenly a masked figure lunged at him with a "boo ". He grappled with it and threw him to the ground. The figure pulled off his mask...just a teenager...

"Hey mister! "

He backed away, stammering apologies and strode further through the labyrinthine passageway.

"Where are you? You can't escape me devil..."

"You can't escape me devil! "a voice mimicked him, mockingly.

He struck the wall with frustration and suddenly a figure launched from the shadows, latching onto him with sharp claws and grabbing his locks like a bridle. The hobgoblin tore at his cheeks, lacerating him with talons and serrated fangs, his prey unable to dislodge him...The other hobgoblins cheered him on.

Mr. Elmer burst out of the haunted house to the screams of the crowd...

The hobgoblins mingled with the crowd and before they could flee, reassured them eagerly.

"Don't be alarmed. It's all part of the show! Pass it on..."

"Yes! It's all part of the show," They chorused.

Alarmed screams turned to laughter and cheers...

"Wow all that blood looks so real..."

He reeled into the street, finally casting the hobgoblin off.

"How positively unceremonious of thee...Hey!"

Mr. Elmer's hands finally grasped the Sceptre....

"Alas! Unhand it at once! Tis the mistress's sceptre..." The hobgoblin objected.

With a roar began to tear it out of the hobgoblin's grasp....

Yet just as it started to slip through his fingers, a she-hobgoblin leapt in and sank her fangs into his wrist. He cried out in agony and again the hob goblin bounded away with sceptre. He drew back from them as the other goblins advanced on him like a troupe of ghoulish jesters...

He had to escape. He would recover the sceptre later surely...but now he must flee...As he retreated, they herded him down the dark and strangely abandoned streets cackling like a pack of hyenas pursuing a wounded prey relentlessly.

Where were all the crowds.... the hordes of visitors...? Mr. Elmer wondered.

In the distance he heard the boom of music and a roar of appreciation at a debuting act. That crowd would help him surely...

He ran past leering skeletons and witches gloating from each branch towards the safety of a crowd... He burst into their midst and he was lost in the kaleidoscopic swirl of masked faces as if stirred in a seething cauldron.

The blaring music drowned out his cries as a band dressed in outlandish gothic attire and faces painted likes skulls played their danse macabre wildly. They joined hands and danced in a circle around him, drums beating...tempo quickening in climax to a ritual.

To his horror, there on the stage was the mime, beckoning for him.

They prodded him with pitchforks.

"Bring him forth..." She signed.

They passed him over their heads and cheered, chanting his name...

"She's a witch!" He cried.

They cheered.

"No! A real one! Witches are real!"

"Are you a witch, too?"

"No."

They booed.

The bell in the old colonial steeple tolled as the crowd him back towards the stage...

Coloured smoke rose amid crimson strobe light. Figures chanting his name, silhouetted against the stage lights. The bands played feverishly.

"Any last things you wish to say?"

A microphone was lowered to his lips.

"I am innocent! Innocen-"

"Boo! "

An executioner drumroll beat, yet to heavy metal. Dark-hooded figures flanked the band, gripping torture brands and prongs that were smouldering red. The stage began to sink into the ground as they played and his screams became shrieks of agony. The crowds cheered and danced wildly; their shadows cast gigantically on the old buildings in eerie revel. She stepped off the stage cradling her cat, seemed to pass intangibly through the crowd as they chanted his name.

She reached out her hand towards his mouth and tongue. She tore his tongue out by the root. It seemed to writhe like the severed head of a reptile or eel in cold-blood death throes. The tongue that pronounced death on so many and transplanted it into her own mouth. He heard a voice that he thought he had silenced forever.

"I swore before you took my tongue, I'd return for you, that I'd hunt you down in the city you once ruled as tyrant. "

Muted himself now, he ran. The jack o lanterns posted along the way ignited in succession and ventriloquised screams in his own voice...Suddenly he collided with an invisible barrier...he tried to draw back, but found his arms ensnared...He thrashed against it, yet found himself further entwined...with sickening realisation he realised he was caught in a giant spiderweb hung like a ghostly banner from the trees in front of the old cemetery...

"Have we served thee well mistress?"

"Aye that ye have..." She lowered the sceptre of Hades on his shoulder like an accolade.

"May we feed then mistress...?"

Like spiders drawn by the vibrations of struggling prey figures crawled across from the corners of the web to gorge...

"Hail witch finder of Salem! Oh hail to thee!" The hobgoblin prodded him with the sceptre...

Skeletal hands flowing with dirt as they rose like carnivorous plants pointed accusing fingers at him. He screamed as he was devoured alive by piranha like mouths as the goblin howled with laughter....

Blame it on the Pumpkin

"Happy Halloween!! O Happy Halloween indeed!!!"

They gorged like leeches and swarmed him to scavenge like nocturnal scavengers making grotesque slurping sounds as they fed.

Days later in aftermath, street crews cleared the Halloween props and decorations. A clean-picked skeleton was cut from a red spiderweb and packed into a crate with other holiday decorations...

The day after Halloween, the doors of the historic house were cast open to waiting tour groups and there she stood, smiling hospitably. She was introduced to a crowd of eager visitors.

"Please give a warm Salem welcome to our new docent...she is joining us from Ireland. Yes, please make her feel welcome...in the wake of Mr. Elmer's mysterious absence we have hired a new hostess...A former acquaintance of Mr. Elmer's no less.... I am sure you will be as impressed by her equally uncanny ability to make history come alive.... "

"Yes, welcome to Salem." She beamed with a lilting brogue.

"Where witches rule!" An enthusiastic visitor beamed.

She smiled.

Blame it on the Pumpkin

Trick or Treat: Once Upon a Hunter's Moon

By Greg Patrick

"Listen to them, the children of the night. What music they make!" — Bram Stoker, Dracula

As if a mysterious circus caravan, rolled into town while the inhabitants slept, the leaf-strewn street of the quaint picturesque village seemed to transform overnight in ghoulish metamorphosis. Eyes blearily opened from nightmares were greeted by a riotous necropolis of skulls grinning and witches cackling at every corner and lamppost. Between the phantasmagoria of lavishly witch-festooned houses lit welcomingly to bands of trick or treaters, was a dark gap where a long-abandoned Victorian mansion, a gaunt shadow of its former stately grandeur...slowly rotted. It was shunned of course, hurried past its long shadow to another comfortingly lit house.

Then an enigmatic stranger from the western states, it was said, moved in... A certain "Mr. Elmer." He remained reclusive, spurning curious eyes and neighborly overtures at welcome....all until one infamous All Hallows eve...

That infamous night when the rivalry between neighbors at the greatest Halloween display would be upstaged at a gargantuan scale....In that tranquil town "where nothing happened."

"Quite a display there..." a cheery voice jarringly intruded into the brooding of that architect of palatial shrine to all things ghostly. An awkward but amicable postman remarked, startling him from his brooding and elaborate final touches...

"Mail?" he asked.

"Yes sir. Just making my rounds. You must be Mr. Elmore..."

"His groundskeeper" he replied evasively.

"Oh...Nobody's seen the fellow since he moved in to the old place....reclusive soul I guess..."

"Apparently" he replied dismissively.

"Fact is I'm surprised anyone would move into the place...with its history and all..."

"Oh?" he asked suddenly intrigued.

The house was built over the burnt ruins of an old witch's haven in the woods.

Legend has it the witches would steal corpses from the old graveyard and tried to raise them to life. Some say they were successful...Then the old reverend came at the head of a mob and burnt the place down...This house was built over it...Nobody who's moved in has stayed long. They say the witches and whatever spells they worked never really left...I guess the real estate agent didn't say nuthin' about it...I'd imagine that charming anecdote was tactfully neglected...But anyway a man like his house needs his secrets..."

"What?" he asked alarmed.

"Oh nuthin'...Well anyway if you see Mr. Elmore please give my regards...and his mail. Thanks Mr...."

"Good day" he replied curtly turning away.

Mr. Elmer had sought exile here...years that seemed centuries past...yet he was the same...beneath the façade...beneath the mask...something lycanthropic was betrayed in his eyes...

The longer nights closed in...his sleep was haunted by strange dreams...and he thought of them again...as if they stood at his bedside...rather than bound and covered in the basement...his past...three...

No. That was not entirely true...there was another...Executed while protesting his innocence to the last...He left that town after that...moved away from that place...

He felt no remorse...none saw his guilt. He saw to that...He was always so careful...The plan was perfect, exile to another place...Hide among strangers...It was perfect...

And yet...

The old hungers called to him like cries in the night...He would leave here too...yes...But not before there was a fifth...

"It's been so long" he thought.

He sharpened his old axe by the hearth and stashed it carefully behind an antique bookshelf. The night was marked with a red smile on the calendar. Halloween. He smiled.

Night cast its dark spell falling as black as dreamless sleep over the row of gabled roofs leading to the old colonial churchyard. He had overslept in his nap before his grand opening...

The dream was the same...as the night wind seemed to sing a carol at his window.

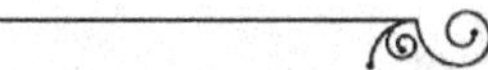

The persistent knocking again...He rose with a grunt to fling the door open...it was already ajar...He was drawn like a sleepwalker as he looked out from his doorstep...before him a display of pumpkins ignited, their skull like eyes flaring. They leered fire at him as he lurched forward. As if ventrloquised by the eerie moan of the wind, the pumpkins chanted: "Guilty! Guilty!"

And silhouetted against the crimson smiles, four dark featureless figures waited. The carved eyes smoldered like nocturnal creatures.

He awoke with a start...

He took out his axe and brought it down on a lit jack o lantern.

"Nothing will stop me tonight do you hear me?"

Doors were cast open and the streets were overrun by a wild menagerie of little ghouls...People waited hospitably eager to be graced with all manners of ghosts and ghouls...

"Trick or treat..."

Trick or treat..."

Yet strangely the anticipated knocks never came...Their houses were bypassed as the children stampeded to one glowing beacon...That Halloween "witch manor" was gloriously reopened.

Towering over the dreamscape of houses were lit in eerie splendour for Halloween like gothic birthday cakes enticing masked hordes from the dark, the house was lit resplendently enticingly...like a giant enticing witch's Gingerbread house...

Like a dashing showman basking in centerstage was the once reclusive Mr. Elmer...His radiant home besieged by hordes of goblins...little hands snapping at his seemingly endless cauldron of candy...And he lavished them with candy and cakes...and they came in waves...Like insatiable piranha mouths their little hands snapped up the candy and delicacies the masked faces swirling around kaliedsocopically in a wild danse macabre...

A skull-masked boy smiled up at him and Mr. Elmer smiled back patronizingly...*A fixed smile like that carved on a jack o lantern...*Yet his eyes betrayed an uneasiness as he looked beyond the tide of ghouls...To four figures standing aloof from the revelry....

They were silhouetted ephemerally against the display of jack o lanterns...Perhaps an older youth escorting children...They ventured no closer.... Wavering in intent vigil, motionless as shadows cast by the interplay of light.

He forced a wider smile that split his lip and wiped a trickle of blood as he beckoned to them hospitably with an affable wave...yet the figures dissolved eerily in a sudden gust of wind and mist like a cauldron's vapors...the shroud of mist seeped between the jostling children and they inhaled the darkness and spectral mist...A spasmodic shudder swept through the crowd like an impact ripple over a dark sea...

Mr. Elmer didn't notice...His eyes never left the place where the ghostly strangers stood... Before they dematerialized he beheld them illuminated In the crimson glow of the lanterns...by the mischievous Interplay of light...Recognized their faces...His face grew ashen and he recoiled....He felt a surge of unease...then fear....

He suddenly gasped...feeling a sharp pain on his hand...He raised it inspectingly...*Bitten?* The hands grabbed quicker at the candy...More rapaciously...then clawing at an empty bottom in disbelief...Their eyes looked up at him hungrily. Then a collective yelp of disbelief rose from their ranks...

"Trick or treat!" they chanted.

"Trick or treat!!"

The voices must have been amplified by the walls, he thought...

Those weren't children's voices...Their monstrous faces glared up at him...Hands raised and grasping...He drew back suddenly...Their eyes smoldered with hunger like nocturnal creatures...

He reeled back against the onslaught...and slammed the door. He staggered back into the living room turning off the lights with grim finality...He knocked over spare boxes of candy stacked to the door before sinking into his armchair....

The chanting persisted as they pumped broomsticks and pitchforks in the air.

This wasn't right....wasn't natural. Their behavior turned darker...

He screamed as a figure of a boy dressed as a skeleton launched to the windowsill and pressed suddenly against the mullioned windows, skeletal hands clawing at the panes. Mr. Elmer saw the faces of others behind him, eyes smoldering emberously.

"Trick or treat! Trick or treat!" they roared.

He buried his face in his hands.

"I should call the police...yes. Yes. No....no I can't...The basement...the basement...my secret...." Then he heard it...*the knocking...*

Not from the front door, he realized with sickening realization...*The basement door...*

"Trick or treat" the chant continued, growing in immensity as if the night itself chanted.

He rose shaking...He took up his old axe, threw the books aside to find it...He rose and followed the sounds in the dark...

"You remember this axe he snarled don't you?" he growled. He dropped the axe then...The basement hatch was ajar...The chains and bolts torn off as if something inside ripped its way out, like cage bars too frail to hold back wild animals.

He reeled back, backed away, picking up and then dropping the axe from trembling hands then...He froze as he heard a child's voice behind him, like venomed honey...a little girl dressed as a witch was framed at the threshold...

"Trick or treat...trick or treat...." she rasped.

He heard scrambling and scurrying as the candy scattered and was snapped up voraciously as they overran his house. They were chattering like animals in a feeding frenzy...less like a mob than a pack of carnivorous animals...

He backed away, fumbling for his axe...And for a place to hide...

They were too distracted by the candy...

He backed into a boy costumed as a skeleton.

"Over here...the offering is here!" he crowed.

They pursued him through the house...He had turned off the lights, yet he sensed with sickening realization that they would find him in the darkness...He heard them advancing...their footfalls and chattering sounded insect like...

He dove under a table and crawled into a ball, cowering and trembling...Time elapsed...a frenzy of searching...the sounds of broken vases and chairs...then silence...

They've gone....surely they've gone...

He dared open his eyes...And there, head hanging down, was a small skull-masked face mocking him with a grisly smile...

"Trick or treat!" he hissed.

"Give us something good to eat!"

He was grasped and violently pulled out from beneath and clutched by hundreds of hands...

"Trick or treat!" they chanted.

He was lifted onto the table, like it was an altar, and borne on top of it, out of the house in ghoulish torch-lit procession.

"Trick or treat! Trick or treat!"

"Where are you taking me?!?"

"To the cemetery of course!" the skull boy squealed jubilantly.

They poked him with pitchforks and gloated at his horror. The old wrought iron gate screeched open before them. They lowered the table in a circle of vandalized statues. The heads of majestic marble angels had been replaced by Jack o lanterns that the children lit like profane idols. Their burning grins leered down from winged torsos.

"Prepare Her treat!"

"Trick or treat! Trick or treat!" they chanted incessantly.

They forced a candied apple in his mouth and a pig mask on his face. His arms were bound and splayed across the table...

They chanted then in a strange language...

"The ritual! The ritual!" they screeched in feverish anticipation. Some grasped candles, others cavorted wildly in a circle...their monstrous shadows cast on the church wall. The witch-masked girl hopped onto the table, cackling...

She raised a carving knife like a sacrificial dagger to the thrill of the gloating masked faces, chattering like nocturnal insects...She pulled down her mask to reveal an angelic face.

"Accept our offering..."

"Hasten sister! Hasten for the hour draws nigh... Hasten...!" the skull-masked boy begged.

She chanted a strange incantation.

They joined hands then in a great circle like an immense serpent coil.

"Trick or treat!" "Trick or treat! Give us something good to eat!" Their voices rose in shrill chorus.

"Trick or treat! Trick or treat!"

He screamed at the falling blade, yet it was drowned out by their chant.

Hundreds of slavering mouths and claws leaning in, teeth bared to feed voraciously...Little party cups were raised like chalices collecting the streaming red. The little "witch" licked the blade as if from a carved cake.

"Trick or treat!" they howled in wild rapture like a pack of wolves over a kill.

Then the bells from the old colonial church tolled midnight...

Like an exorcised spirit a dark mist was exhaled from their mouths, morphing into a grisly spectral figure like a harpy before shifting amorphously and dissipating like a receding tide between the graves.

A spasmodic shudder swept the horde, that sent them to the ground...The children rose taking of their masks and staggered, dazed...bleary eyed and disoriented as if from a nightmare...

"Mommy!" a little girl began to cry...

And confronting the old witch's house, four figures reappeared as if restless shadows were granted form and face...They lingered against a background of dozens of displayed jack o lanterns like an eerie shrine...They raised their arms like a coven of witches in the act of conjuring and the disembodied moan of the wind caressed them as the Jack o lanterns were suddenly extinguished at the final tolling of the bell.

Meanwhile as frantic parents were reunited with their children wandering aimlessly in the dark, the kindly old churchyard caretaker approached a sobbing child.

"Goodness you are out late...You should run along home then...There, there. Don't cry....my you have been busy tonight".

He looked at his amply filled bag...

"And what did you get for trick or treat?"

Reluctantly the child reached into the bag and Mr. Elmer's severed head was raised by its hair, candy spilling from its mouth.

Blame it on the Pumpkin

THE HALLOWEEN SEANCES

By E. W. Farnsworth

Four old girlfriends sat in their costumes waiting for the medium to begin the séance. Buckets were strategically placed all over the floor of the leaky barn, and the pucks and plops of drippings brought the wild thunderstorm alive inside as thunder and lightning played havoc with outdoor festivities. As the young women grew accustomed to the horror of their surroundings, they began to talk nervously.

"This is certainly no night for trick-or-treating," said Melinda Foster, who hated sitting every Halloween on a high stool by her door in her witch costume with bowls of candy for the endless procession of "brats." She had turned her lights off to signal no treats were available tonight before she padded through the rain runoff to the barn.

Nancy Distal howled with laughter, her octopus tentacles shaking all over her body and head. "It's cold and drafty in here. Every time the lightning strikes I see things in the far reaches of this building, and the thunder makes my stomach churn. When is the séance going to begin? I think I just felt a drop from the ceiling run down my back. It makes my skin crawl."

Holly Porton waved her right paw. She was unrecognizable in her wookie costume except she was the tallest of the four and her fur was symbolic. "Matilda will be starting any minute now. Nancy, is that one of your tentacles groping up my thigh."

"Ladies, be civil—and patient. Arranging this spiritual event in the medium's busiest season was chancy and expensive." The voice of reason and equanimity, Lucille Manning had a calming effect on the others—and her gossamer outfit studded with sequins made her shine in the dim candlelight. "If you look closely when the storm flashes, you'll notice the spiders' webs in the rafters are not fake but real."

Melinda nodded in agreement. "I would not be surprised if itsy bitsy spiders crawled all over us while we are trying to commune with the dead."

After a short interval of close-by, crackling thunder, the medium made her grand entrance and proceeded in stately fashion to her chair at the table, dropping her cigarette to the barn floor and stamping it out with her boot. A black-haired gypsy, the older woman took her time making herself comfortable while she set her crystal ball in the center of the table and laid her Tarot card deck to her right side. "Before I begin, I must ask whether you brought the money we agreed on."

Lucille stood and passed the bag with the cash across to Matilda Rinaldi, who wasted no time taking out the bills and counting them—three times, slowly. When she was satisfied her count was right, she put the bills back into the bag and hid it beneath her dress. She brushed herself off before she brought out from under her dress a thick red candle and a tiny red plate. She put the candle on the plate and lighted the wick with a Swan Vesta wooden match. The candlelight gave off a dull red glow in contrast to the white light of five thick, plain candles strategically positioned on stanchions behind the five oak chairs around the table.

"For those who are new to a séance, you will remain silent and reverent unless you feel moved or the spirits address you by name. You are all in costume, so I will assume you are making statements: a witch, a wookie, a harem concubine and a Cthulhu devotee. I came as I always am—a gypsy queen. I shall first consult the Tarot cards."

Matilda dealt five cards to the five points of the pentagram star inscribed in the surface of the table. The Fool, the Madman, the Sorcerer, the Knight and Death appeared in order. Now she dealt three cards face down in the center. "Please examine the card that lies nearest to you. Think deeply and take the image to the depths of your soul. When you are ready to proceed, look up at me and nod."

The gypsy practiced what she preached, peering at Death with fierce intensity for almost five minutes before looking up.

The five women relaxed somewhat as they performed this exercise. The storm continued outside, and rain ran down the gutters and spouts that lined the barn while under the eaves, the wind whistled and the wood of the barn creaked in the darkness like a ghost ship lost at sea. An owl swooped down and flew around under the interior eaves before it flew upward and roosted out of sight. The sound of dripping remained incessant while the candles' light changed as the drafts swung this way and that.

Matilda knocked her knuckles on the table. Each of her four guests did likewise. "Now we shall hold the hands of the persons to our right and left. No matter what happens, no one will release the handholds till our séance has been completed. Look into the red candle's flame. Do not divert your eyes even if a draft extinguishes the flame."

The fire danced on the tip of the wick. The women became comfortable with their handholds. Matilda began to chant, at first unintelligibly. Then her singing became an incantation.

"Spirit spectators, always abiding, come forth to make yourselves known."

Matilda hesitated, as if she were waiting for a sign.

"I sense your reluctance. Be not afraid." The owl came down from her rafter and landed in the center of the oak table on top of the three cards. Her head swiveled slowly stopping as if to capture the features of each woman around the table. Then she expanded her enormous wings and took off, returning to her perch.

Though the rustling of the spooky creature's feathers raised goose bumps on the women's arms, they abided by the medium's instructions: no one broke her handhold or diverted her eyes from the red candle's flame.

"Spirits! You witness us waiting patiently. Your messenger owl has been your harbinger. Now come forth yourselves."

An enormous black widow spider dropped onto the table after hanging from its black web and when it landed, it turned in a slow, counterclockwise circle. The poisonous arachnid walked confidently across each of the five Tarot cards with their faces up, and she came to rest on the smiling rictus of Death.

Matilda asked the spider, "Do you wish to speak or remain silent, Spirit?"

The black widow moved from the mouth to the hollow right eye of Death.

"Someone here has suffered a most grievous loss. The spirit of the departed comes to console." The witch wept quietly, her tears falling on the card for the Fool. Matilda did not interrupt the woman's grieving.

The black widow advanced, but a green serpent appeared on the table from below it and snapped the spider down without ceremony. As the snake's mouth crushed the life out of the black widow, it coiled and writhed as it sought the next card where it curled on its back over the Madman.

Matilda said, "A second spirit has entered this sacred pentagonal space. It has mighty powers. Madness too has power, and this spirit knows how fragile minds afflicted with Alzheimer's can crush a family's equanimity. Now was the wookie's time to cry. Her tears fell on the card in front of her but she refrained from speaking. The green snake brushed against her sleeve before slithering to the next card: the Sorcerer. The snake's forked tongue flicked out of its mouth repeatedly, its bright black eyes searching for prey. An enormous crash of thunder broke the women's fascination with the snake.

The gypsy queen said, "I now see Aladdin in his sailor suit, his muscled, crossed arms and chest glistening with scented oil. With the snap of his fingers, he conjures a lamp with burning whale oil. Tell us, Spirit, why you have come to this meeting?"

The thunder rolled like ninepins in a celestial bowling alley. Matilda interpreted her vision: "The sailor has retreated, but not before he signaled to another spirit."

A broad-winged bat flittered around the ladies' heads as if looking for a nesting place. While the bat played from one coiffure to another fleetingly, the owl returned to grab the green snake in its talons and fly to its roost making eerie "who-who" owl sounds. The bat landed on the table and walked like a miniature, winged human to the Knight card and looked the costumed Cthulhu figure in the eye. Then it leapt up and took flight. It flew about frantically in circles, gyring ever upward toward the ceiling where it finally hung from a rafter alongside its family.

The medium interpreted, "So we have had four spirits visit, only the last was with us briefly. The knight stands stalwart and unmoved, aloof and silent. So all four spirits are ready for the audience. Whoever wants to address her spirit may do so now, freely in any order."

The witch said, "You were always the fool, right till the day you expired. You lost all our money, and I had to go back to work. You took the easy path and left me alone and defenseless. Now you come to offer consolation, but I am inconsolable by you as you betrayed me. Yet I am glad I had this chance to tell you what I thought."

The concubine spoke next. "You, standing like a magician from some fabulous tale, abandoned me, so I was left alone to seek delight in the arms of others. You were the genie I found, but you did not stay with me. My broken heart is all I have left of you, and now I am everyman's one-woman harem. Judge me not since you left me no good options."

When she spoke, the wookie was weeping again. "Your mind went so quickly, it confused us all, me most because we had grown so close. Now I wonder whether in your spirit guise you can understand how much I loved you and how much I grieved for your loss before you left me forever. Now I do not shave my legs in repentance for all I could not do for you alive."

For a long while, the figures at the table remained silent in the cold as the candles flickered in the drafts. Then the Cthulhu figure spoke in a sententious, authoritative voice. "Those with power cannot divulge their weaknesses without losing it. You were a captain of industry, and I was your muse. Even when I saw disaster coming and warned you, you refused to believe me. Was it your resentment of my second sight? Did you hope to overcome the obdurate obstacles I foresaw? Now we are past the hope of peace, and I have my visions still, but they are less vivid now you have gone. Woe has taken your place, and I weep."

Matilda sat for a long time in silence as her customers adjusted to the effects of their shared experience. The red candle was now half the size it had been at the séance's commencement. The storm seemed to have passed. Dripping continued into a score of wooden and zinc buckets. The sounds of owls feeding and nestling came from the barn's ceiling.

The gypsy queen released her handholds, thus freeing the others to do the same. Matilda calmly pulled her Tarot cards together. She blew out the red candle and let the wax cool before she placed the candle and plate under her clothing. She also retrieved her crystal ball and hid it under her garments. Without a word, she rose and departed the barn leaving the four women still sitting around the table in a recovery state.

Melinda, the witch, was first to speak. "Is that all the séance was to have offered?"

"You were expecting personal catharsis, perhaps?" Lucille asked, but not unkindly.

Holly, the wookie, said, "I, for one, got what we bargained for—a credible version of truth. And no one can say the gypsy knew beforehand what was going to transpire."

Nancy stood up carefully as she had all her tentacles waving about. She turned on her cell phone and looked at the time announced, "Ladies, it is now 11:59 pm. Lucille, this Halloween is about to pass."

Lucille, the concubine, smiled and stood. "Yes, the séance is over, and so is the raging storm. We should all go home, as it will be safe outside now that All Saints Day has come. As a precaution, though, you might want to check your hair for nesting bats and brush any spiders off your clothing."

Holly said, "It's only a short walk home in any case. But we should walk together as long as possible!"

As the four widows emerged from the barn, the moonlight was breaking through the parting clouds. A cool breeze was cutting through the woods around their suburban complex, and the women shivered. In a distant tree, an owl hooted, and the woods were full of scuffling sounds of unknown predators and prey playing out their primeval games.

*

For the three years prior to the séance, the four young women had been inseparable. They belonged to the same neighborhood association and the same country club. They even shared the same psychiatrist. Their visit to the séance in the barn was their first communal paranormal adventure, and after the first one, they vowed to make Madam Matilda Rinaldi their medium of choice for Halloweens thereafter.

"I am still marveling at how 'spot on' Matilda was about all of us—and she had no special knowledge or briefing on anyone." Lucille took another bite of her cucumber sandwich and saw her friends nodding in agreement. It was early summer, and they were all dressed in their spandex bikinis at a poolside table at their club. Any of them might have walked off the runway of a local modeling agency as they had great figures and kept themselves well, except for Holly, who was still not shaving her legs as a symbol of fidelity to her deceased husband.

Nancy sipped her Pinot Grigio and began praising an Asian massage parlor she had frequented last Thursday. She had the others sitting at the edge of their chairs as they vicariously experienced the massage she described with her.

"Well, I am sold," said Melinda when her friend had finished her pitch. "I am going to make an appointment at the spa this afternoon. Shall I make appointments for all of us, or not?"

"Leave me out for now," Holly said. The others looked at her legs and got pained looks on their faces. "I am looking forward to Duplicate Bridge this Saturday."

Lucille said, "I am looking forward to competing as well. Out of curiosity, has anyone changed his life style since the séance?"

The women looked at each other in surprise. Nancy said, "What kind of changes did you think might happen?"

"Well, the séance was the first event that touched us all to the core at the same moment. We each revealed something intimate and important if not essential about ourselves during the event. Sometimes such an epiphany or self-realization, can lead to big changes. I am just curious."

Melinda said, "Lucille, have you noticed any changes in your own behavior since then?

Lucille ran her long finger around the rim of her wineglass and said, "As a matter of fact, I have, but it's more like a deep feeling than a behavioral change."

"Are you going to keep us in suspense or reveal it, Lucille?"

"Well, Melinda, I have been thinking of limiting my dating range to a single man."

Nancy said, "Whoa! Sister, that's front-page news. Who is the lucky man? And why haven't you told us about him before in these terms?"

Lucille blushed. "It seemed to me I have been playing the field to all comers far too long. That was okay for a while. And I felt I was being true to my husband in the process, but I felt empty inside, for all the flattering external attentions. After the séance I knew I should settle down and focus on one man. Fernando Lopez is that man."

Holly blurted out, "Who the blazes is Fernando Lopez? You have never mentioned the name to us, have you?"

"No, Holly, I have not. Fernando is a wildly successful plastic surgeon—one of the best within five hundred miles. He is handsome, rich and a terrific lover. Lately, he has been most attentive to me, and he is making all the right noises as a prelude to proposing marriage."

"Well, that's worth a toast!" Nancy said, raising her glass. "Here's to Lucille's new lasting relationship. May they endure 'the slings and arrows of outrageous fortune' and achieve happiness!" The women all drank to that sentiment.

For a long time afterward, the women harbored their private thoughts. Something about their friend's look of confidence made them wonder why they had not felt the same. Lucille was the natural leader of the group, and naturally they felt inclined to examine their own lives. The idea Fernando might change the dynamics of their group permanently made them anxious. Nancy wondered out loud whether Lucille's relationship might end their foursome forever.

"After all, we hardly knew each other when we were married. Only after our husbands passed did we come together. I fear as we pick our mates, we will hew to them and forget each other entirely.

"Nancy, you are being ridiculous. Let's see how things go before we fly into a panic."

Yet Nancy, who was genuinely psychic, had a premonition. Lucille's romance with Fernando was a whirlwind affair, and two weeks after she first mentioned his name to her friends at their club, she was wearing the surgeon's enormous diamond engagement ring. One week later, she brought her catch to lunch at the club where he swam in his skimpy spandex suit and showed off his washboard stomach and arm muscles. Lucille announced their June wedding plans, to be followed by a two-week honeymoon to the island of Gozo in the Mediterranean Sea.

Holly told Nancy that Fernando was the image of Aladdin in the séance, but she would not countenance any connection of the imminent marriage to the Halloween event. The four friends worked together to make the wedding a complete success—with Lucille's three friends serving as Maids of Honor and Fernando's three handsome brothers as the ring bearers.

In the run-up to the wedding, Nancy noticed Holly had shaved her legs. This was such a stunning change, the friends staged a celebration lunch poolside for the entire wedding company. Bringing such attention to Holly made the others extremely careful of their own appearances. Fernando's brothers were not slack about picking out their favorites. So Michel, Pietro and Sergio began dating Melinda, Nancy and Holly. By the time of the wedding, not one but four Lopez marriages were in prospect.

Once again, Nancy's psychic consciousness saw consistencies between the individual men and details of the Halloween séance, but this time she held her peace as she was falling head over heels in love with Pietro and she did not want to upset any plans made by the others.

The first marriage went like a charm. Lucille and Fernando looked seraphic in their costumes. After the reception, they flew off to Gozo for their honeymoon. Lucille had promised to be back in time to help plan the next three weddings, and Fernando volunteered to pay for everything his brothers needed to make their nuptials as pleasant as his had been.

The three men and women got along famously as couples and as a group. When Lucille and Fernando returned from their honeymoon with the highest praise for Gozo as a honeymoon destination, the other brothers all opted to follow the same route as their elder brother And his bride. With that decided, Fernando bought an estate on Gozo where the honeymoons could take place. He staffed the place with an island man-and-wife team to cater to his brothers' every need.

By September, the four couples had all been wed, and Fernando's estate on Gozo had become a family-favorite destination. Lucille importuned her husband to buy the barn wherein the séance had occurred and the four nearby suburban properties the women owned as well. He was once again totally immersed in his plastic surgery business, so he was glad to have an active partner in the fundamental decisions about the family.

For her part, Lucille never asked about her husband's plastic surgery business. She knew his trade was lucrative and so highly technical the barriers to entry for any would-be competitors were impossibly high. In fact, though, other reasons made his business untouchable, but she did not discover those until much later.

Blame it on the Pumpkin

The relationships of the four men and women were on the surface strong and loving. Money was never a problem, but Fernando's brothers often had to spend long periods abroad for work. After their absences, they returned with such insatiable desires, their women not only forgave them but they even looked forward to the "rest intervals" they would have before their next excursions. Children arrived in the second and third years and in all the following ten years. The "Lopez Dynasty" became a term with meaning behind it.

Living in close proximity, the four women remained true to their former friendships, and they shared information constantly about their uncommon family. Every year on Halloween, the four women went to the barn for their annual séance. At Lucille's insistence, nothing about the edifice had been changed. The same holes in the roof required the same buckets to collect any moisture. The owls and bats in the rafters were allowed to remain in place. The spiders and snakes had their own way of keeping alive. And then there were proliferating mice and rats.

Matilda Rinaldi was happy to provide her services as a medium, but at in increased rate each time. As before, she insisted on counting her cash payment before she commenced her supernatural service. For continuity, the four friends always wore the same costumes as they had done on their first visit. Naturally, the Tarot cards were different from those the medium dealt before, and the manifestations of the invoked spirits were different too.

The differences were not subtle. Instead of images of The Madman and Death were images of The Queen of Wands, The Ace of Cups and The World. The spirits morphed from the four gentlemen who had been the former husbands of the four widows to the parents, grandparents and ancestors of the Lopez brothers. The fruitfulness of the women and the wealth of the family were now the medium's major themes.

The four women each had borne three children by the end of the fifth year. A portion of the land around the barn had been converted to a garden and playground for the growing Lopez family. Doctor Lopez's business seemed to be going better than ever before though

Lucille wished he would take some time off to restore himself.

"Husband, don't we have enough riches to allow you a few days' leisure once a while?"

He raised an eyebrow. "Everything we have could be gone in an instant. I must keep active or my clients will lose faith in me. As things sit now, the competition has no chance to break my control. I don't have to remind you how we have struggled to build what we have."

Lucille was an intelligent woman. She could not fathom any of her husband's competitors capable of horning in on his business. Still, she did not argue. She was concerned about her husband's health, but she was also devoted to his happiness. Besides, she had to console her three friends for the long absences their own husbands endured for their labors though none of the women knew what their work consisted of.

In small bits the scope of the Lopez brothers' labors became apparent. Only the eldest was a top-earning surgeon. The others were businessmen engaged in international commerce. Their separate enterprises were underwritten by the surgeon's assets, which consisted of real estate, stocks and bonds, cryptocurrencies and cash reserves. An old family maxim, "Buy for one and sell for two" covered the bulk of their businesses and allowed them to expand what they were doing almost in any direction.

One example stood out among many: the trade in fresh cut flowers. Pietro Lopez discovered how to fill orders during a shortage. By using the family accounts as leverage, he made a fortune doing what none of the normal wholesale vendors had the wherewithal to accomplish. He did not make the mistake of remaining in the flower trade beyond the time of the crisis of supply. When he had made his final flower deliveries, he paid off all his creditors, including his borrowings from family, and went looking for other ventures.

Michel was also enterprising but in a different way. His favorite story was about finding seven refrigerator railroad cars full of swine carcasses, which he bought for a fifth of the going rate while he found a buyer looking for pork at any price. By putting together the deal, he made a small fortune for the family. He did not look to repeat his success. Instead, he thought long and deep about shortages of lumber as the global economy started a new boom phase. He used his earnings from the pork sales to buy lumber futures, which were still in a slump. He waited till the lumber market made its inevitable turn upward and sold his contracts for seven times the value he bought them for. Now he was looking for new pastures.

Sergio was not letting his brothers pull all the freight for their family's fortune. Quietly, he bought raw land throughout America in ten-to-forty-acre parcels. His choices were not random as some looked like good mining prospects while others offered potential rights of way for pipelines or exclusive hunting rights for the super-wealthy. By buying and selling raw land, he avoided taxes on improvements while selling at reasonable profits and churning his money into other land holdings.

The Lopez brothers were careful not to boast about their wealth. They did not drive flashy cars, and they encouraged their wives to be frugal. As Lucille thought things through, she discerned patterns that were built to last. She felt increasingly comfortable working with only a little of her husband's wealth. She used her seamstress skills to make the children's clothing. She harvested fruits, spices and vegetables from her hand-tilled garden. She encouraged thrift in her three friends and shared what she had with a glad heart.

Things were going so well for the Lopez family, they began to think they had solved all the perennial problems of adversity. And it was not as if ample warning were not available. Matilda Rinaldi's annual Halloween séance portended mysteries, even tragedies, ahead.

In the chilly late night setting of the barn, the four Lopez ladies watched the Tarot cards fall as they had not done in many years. The hanged man was not propitious. Judgment was likewise a caution. The King of Pentacles seemed to harbor the semblance of goodness— at least for the surgeon, but what about the others?

As Matilda Rinaldi went through her routine, her face became pale with worry. The owl scratched Nancy's thumb. The black widow bit Lucille on the back of her hand. The green snake wrapped itself around the crystal ball and would not release the magical sphere even after the séance when Melinda's spells had no apparent effect on the creature. On top of everything else, Holly's hair became the plaything of the bat family: they all flew into her hair and would not come out.

After the medium had gathered her things and departed the barn, Lucille told everyone to stay in their seats to discuss the meaning of the session they had just experienced. She asked her friends to search their memories for any signs of trouble such as their medium had foreseen. Then she asked to be taken to the nearest Emergent Care facility to have her thumb treated for the spider's bite she had received. Nancy, the psychic accompanied her to the medical facility.

While Lucille was being treated, she asked Nancy whether she had any premonitions of disaster as far as their family was concerned.

"It may seem silly, but I did have a dream last week that a gray man was coming to see your husband with very bad news."

"Did you have any idea what the news might be?"

"No, but it was dire—and unexpected. I had the impression our entire world was about to collapse."

Lucille was treated with a topical ointment after the doctor on duty had lanced and cleaned her wounded thumb. At home again, she felt a rising fever and let her mind wander with the idea of the gray visitor.

The next morning, Lucille asked her husband about the gray man, but he said, "We have nothing to worry about. People are always trying to make trouble. I can handle my affairs well enough. You should concentrate on the children and keep them safe." When he kissed her on the neck before he left for his office, she was tempted to do exactly as her husband said, but now she knew Nancy's vision of the gray man had been true to her husband's reality. As she followed her daily routine, she dwelled upon what the gray man meant for the Lopez family's collective future.

A week later, a small, gray man appeared at Lucille's door. She was at first reluctant to allow him entrance, but he seemed so serious she invited him inside for coffee.

"Mrs. Lopez, I approached your husband about the danger he is in, but he would not listen to me. I thought you might talk some sense into the man."

She poured coffee and offered cream and sugar. "I make a habit of not interfering with my husband's business affairs."

"Maybe you should do that on occasion. I am sure you know your husband has a privileged position in his profession."

"I know he is among the best plastic surgeons in the country."

"He is that—and much more. Mrs. Lopez, your husband made a deal long ago to perform special surgical operations under government contract for our witness protection program."

Lucille froze as she contemplated the meaning of what she had just heard. "Assuming what you are saying is true, what can that possibly have to do with my husband's future—and with your appearance before me today?"

"I will come to that in due course. From your facial expression, I can tell you knew nothing about the special nature of your husband's work. You may additionally be unaware of other special work your husband has done since your marriage."

"I have no idea what you are talking about. Perhaps you had better get to the point of your visit."

"Harrumph. Yes, well. I am here to say that your husband's work on our government's special programs is beyond reproach. His extra-curricular operations on the whole are his own business. Our only concern are operations for certain criminals whose changed identities are a crucial matter for security people such as myself."

"Are you telling me my husband has been changing the identities of criminals sought by our government? I must presume these changes have been impenetrable to your experts."

"Yes, that is precisely what I am telling you on both counts."

Mrs. Lopez rose, and the gray man rose as well. "I am sure this is all a great misunderstanding. I have no idea what you want me to do?"

"Given that our coffee is over, I will leave you with a warning. Your husband is in grave danger on account of his secret surgical operations on criminals. If you cannot convince Dr. Lopez to share his private records with my department, he is likely to be terminated by the same criminal organizations for which he worked. Will you try to make him aware of his danger and what he must do? Here is my business card so you can reach me." When the gray man left, Lucille looked at the little man's business card. She almost laughed when she saw the man's name was, "Special Agent Thomas Gray, Security."

That evening after the children went to bed, Lucille decided to have a full and frank exchange with her husband over Cognac.

"What did you do today, Lucille?" he asked.

"Well, aside from the usual, I had a visitor you may know, a Mr. Thomas Gray."

She saw her husband's nose wrinkle. "I can only guess what that little man had to say."

"Among other things, he wanted me to warn you about the dangers you are in for changing the identities of criminals. Specifically, he wanted me to importune you to divulge information from your private records about those operations on criminals he mentioned."

For a while, Dr. Lopez remained extremely quiet. He sipped his drink and closed his eyes while he savored the liquor. "I suppose it was bound to come out eventually."

"What? That you cut criminals so they could not be identified by the authorities?"

"No. That the government would intrude on my wife in her home while I was at work."

"Lucille said, "I don't like the idea you are in danger. I am also afraid for our children and your family. Is there any way we can escape from the threats of these people?"

Lopez looked into her frightened eyes and shook his head slowly. "You have no idea how long the reach of these people is. You can run from them for a while, but you can never hide indefinitely."

"Just maybe, though, we should try. I am game if you are. Think of the children. What about the Lopez estate on Gozo? Or maybe one of the remote properties your brother has collected?"

"For the sake of argument, the whole family must go into hiding all at once. Wherever we go, we must be ready to last through a siege of major proportions—food, water, weapons, ammunition, the works. It would mean massive and permanent disruptions for my brothers and your friends and for all the young ones."

"What are the alternatives to flight?" She was swirling the Cognac in her glass while he prepared an answer.

"After I turn over my private records, I suppose we could stand and fight. The government men and women will try their best to stop the criminals from getting their revenge, but none of them is good enough to eliminate all threats."

"If we stand fast, we can plan to withstand a siege. Does giving Mr. Gray the records really buy us anything?"

"The government is not to be trifled with. By 'opening the kimono,' so to speak, we show good faith. Holding back anything might lead to later resentment and retaliation. I am very sorry I am bringing down the evil people upon our family. I was not aware criminals were behind the operations I was doing—until I had done so many, I was trapped."

"So what are we to do?"

"Tonight, we will get rest. Tomorrow I will gather my private records and deliver them to

Mr. Gray with my request for government protection. I will tell my brothers what is happening. You should tell your friends as well. The criminal organizations might react right away, or they might wait a while to gauge the damage before they retaliate. Does that scare you?"

"Yes, it does. We have all worked so hard to build an estate we can be proud of."

"Once I set the wheels in motion, I will want to make sure our legacy remains intact. You and the others can help me do that."

"I am willing to do whatever is necessary."

"I will give you the keys to our armory in the basement. As we resume our normal lives, I want you to carry a loaded pistol at all times. I also want you to get in touch with your medium for me."

"Matilda Rinaldi, the gypsy woman?"

"Don't be surprised. She has resources beyond your wildest imaginings. Let her know the current situation and let her decide what her role is going to be."

For the next twenty-four hours, Dr. Lopez's plan unfolded in cold, rational terms. He placed his private records in the hands of Mr.

Gray. Lucille contacted the gypsy queen and invited her to tea that afternoon where she laid out the dangerous situation in graphic detail. The gypsy promised to provide security through her enormous Romani family. Meanwhile, the four Lopez brothers had a long lunch whereat they planned for the siege. Finally, in the late afternoon, Lucille and her friends gathered in their private park with the children to discuss the situation and what they planned to do about it.

Matilda Rinaldi joined the women in the park to provide an update.

"My family will be in the background keeping an eye on everything that happens in this neighborhood. They will also be conducting some excavations at the barn including a new strong room below the floor where the entire Lopez family can hide if necessary. Your husband has authorized the build-out, but he wants you to pass judgment on our progress."

"Thank you, Matilda, for your assistance. I am afraid this is going to be a bloody business before it is done."

"Keep cool, Lucille. My gypsies have a long history of surviving oppression. Maybe you can learn from us in that respect."

The government men and women took a long time examining Dr. Lopez's private records. Then they planned and re-planned while they jockeyed to get the funding for their actions. Finally, they began their harvest phase where they found the criminal persons who had received new identities and arrested or killed them. During the so-called harvest phase, the criminal organizations began their own plans for revenge on everyone involved in the upset of their grand scheme. They decided to conduct surveillance of Dr. Lopez and his family.

The Romanis reported increased surveillance on the Lopez neighborhood by unsavory characters, both government types and criminals. The government people took care of the sloppy criminals, leaving the wily criminals to do their worst against the Lopez family. The wily criminals were not averse to using sniper weapons and disguise, but they were no match for the gypsies and their knives. The Lopez neighborhood consequently became a silent battleground, and for a while, the Lopez family remained unscathed. The women used delivery services for groceries and other necessities, and the gypsies did the driving and shopping with daily passwords in the ancient gypsy language.

Meanwhile, the women and children drilled in the park and at the barn so they became familiar with the new underground hiding place and firing positions on all sides. The four Lopez brothers were not idle. They took the fight to the enemy criminal organizations, doing things that the federal authorities were not empowered to do without search warrants and such. In short order, the criminals felt they were under siege and afraid to venture out of their homes for fear of assassination. Mr. Gray became the conduit for the criminals' pleas for protection from the Lopez family. According to what he told Lucille, he marveled at the list of casualties the gangs presented, but he made no promises to extend the government's protection to them without significant confessions to past grievous crimes, which they were never going to deliver.

At an impasse and desiring to return to the good old times before the Lopez betrayal, the big bosses of the crime families called for a truce and used Mr. Gray and his people to broker discussions with the Lopez brothers. So, with white flags flying, the truce meeting was held in the park of the Lopez neighborhood. Several layers of security secured the area surrounding the park, and unmanned airborne surveillance kept watch to the limit of long-rifle range. The upshot of the unprecedented meeting was an agreement to cease hostilities on all sides. The principals made solemn vows and pledges. The government recorded everything that happened with numerous automatic cameras. As an incentive, Mr. Gray stated the government would stop using Dr. Lopez's records in their prosecutions—unless the crime families abandoned the truce, whereupon the government would make war in common cause with the Lopez family against the criminals. No mention was made about the gypsies, who may as well have been invisible participants. The Romanis remained on watch just in case the criminals forgot their oaths.

On the night after the historic truce, Lucille and her husband discussed the situation.

"Dearest husband, you are a genius for having resolved our difficulties!" She touched her wine glass to his and sipped the rich red wine.

"Dearest wife, we do not know how long our truce with the crime families will last."

"At least we have the Romanis to guard us as long as it takes."

"And I will bear the expense of their vigilance. Can you think of anything we might offer Matilda Rinaldi for arranging her family's protection?"

After some thought, Lucille said, "I will ask her what she would like as a special gift from you. It means more to her to have served for honor's sake than to be a mercenary."

Two days later, Lucille was inspecting the barn with Matilda, and she took her chance to discover what the gypsy queen wanted most.

"I almost feel as if I am a member of your family. My clan has taken blood for yours, so in effect, yours and mine are one big family now. I have heard much talk of a great estate your family has in the lush green island of Gozo in the Mediterranean. If the Gypsy King and I could spend a two-week vacation there, we would be satisfied. Understand, we would have to be accompanied by our retainers."

"How many retainers would you wish to accompany you to Gozo?"

"Let's call it fifty, more or less."

Lucille took the word to her husband, who was happy to arrange a chartered flight for the gypsies to Gozo. He tasked his housekeepers there to extend every courtesy to his Romani guests. As not all the gypsies had gone to Gozo, the Lopez family still enjoyed continuous surveillance during the interim.

When the gypsy royalty returned to America, they had nothing but praise for the Lopez family. They proclaimed far and wide that the Lopezes were under special protection for ever.

Fernando Lopez did not relax for one year after the truce. In that time, no threat from the crime families had been evident. Once, he had been approached to do more plastic surgery for the mobsters, but he demurred, suggesting a young upcoming surgeon as a possible provider. Evidently, no offense was taken by the crime family who sought his service. Mr. Gray was gratified at the way the surgeon had handled the situation since he sent a dozen long-stem roses to Lucille as a thank-you present.

The upcoming Halloween was a landmark event as it was the first during which the young children would go trick-or-treating. Only after the children went to bed did the four Lopez women dress in their habitual costumes for their trek to the barn. Thunder and lightning were not evident on this occasion, but a crisp, cold wind sifted the forest and the barn. It whistled under the eaves outside and stirred a commotion within.

The women took their places at four of the points of the pentangle, leaving the chair at the vacant point for the medium. The witch, the wookie, the octopus figure and the concubine got settled though all had goose bumps from the cold. The white candles guttered in the drafts. Above in the eaves were the noises of the owl family and the bats. A green snake slithered up a table leg and coiled itself in the middle of the star symbol.

As if heralding the entrance of the gypsy queen, a single clap of thunder erupted in the cold night sky. Matilda Rinaldi seemed unperturbed as she took her usual place at the table.

She set out her kit of Tarot cards, crystal ball and red plate with red candle and struck a Swan Vesta match to light the wick. The green snake did not stir while she did her preparations.

Matilda did not have to ask for her bag of cash as Lucille had her payment ready. Nevertheless, the medium carefully counted each bill three times to be sure her new rate had been understood. When she had placed the sack with the cash on the special hook she used under her skirt, she dealt five cards around the table and three more next to the green snake in the center.

Now she held out her hands to either side, and the five-sided compact of the women was made. Among them, three mothers were visibly pregnant, and all seemed radiantly happy though their cheeks were reddening from the chill and each was gently shivering.

Lucille noticed The Magician lay on the table in front of her. The Moon was in front of the medium. The Tower was in front of Nancy. The High Priestess faced Melinda. And Holly had drawn Temperance. The women watched the red candle's flame as if mesmerized. A second green snake joined the first one in a dance that took the entire table. The mother owl flew down to take the writhing snakes to her eyrie. The she-bat descended to sniff each coiffure in turn.

The medium broke the silence with the command, "Spirits who inhabit this place, come forth and identify yourselves. I feel your presence within me. Speak if you can, and I will let your voice flow through me."

The gypsy queen was silent as her breath became louder. She moaned and sang an incantation.

"I thrill to hear your voices—four voices in toto. Is it true that you are the former husbands of these visitants? So why have you come tonight?"

She waited for a time. "We have come to bid our former wives goodbye. They have found happiness, which was what we dearly wished. There is nothing left for us to do by way of consolation. Goodbye. Goodbye. Goodbye. Goodbye."

The four former widows wept with a mix of joy and sadness. Each whispered, "Goodbye" to her former mate.

"The four spirits of the departed have vanished. Are there any more spirits around this table tonight? No? Then anyone at this table may say what she wishes without impediment."

Lucille said, "I give thanks from all of us for gifts not yet received."

Nancy nodded, "I have a premonition of birth in beauty in the months ahead."

Holly hesitated to be sure she got things straight. "I am so grateful for shaving my legs."

Finally, Melinda said, "I did not mean it when I said the trick-or-treaters were brats. They are wonderful—and ours were precious making their rounds tonight."

"Ladies, our séance is complete." With that, Matilda assembled her symbols—the cards, the candle with its plate, and the crystal ball—she placed them under her dress and left the barn.

The women sat as if waiting for something else to happen. Then Nancy pulled out her cellphone and announced, "It is now All Saints Day. And it is time for us to go home."

Late to the party was a giant black widow spider, and Lucille slapped the table, smearing the arachnid's carapace across the pentangle. She smiled at having gotten her revenge for a night spent at the Emergent Care. She did not need another such adventure. She was the last to leave the barn, and at the door she ran her hands through her hair lest bats be there. Relieved her tresses were bat free, she followed her sisters through the night by moonlight, satisfied by the outcomes.

ABOUT THE CONTRIBUTORS

MARJORY E. LEPOSKY

Marjory E. Leposky is a filmmaker and children's chapter book author with more than 10 years of production experience on a broad spectrum of projects that include TV commercials, music videos for local artists, and feature film productions.

Marjory earned degrees in television and media production from Miami Dade College formally Miami-Dade Community College and Florida State University.

You can follow Marjory here:

https://www.facebook.com/chatterboxproductions
https://twitter.com/chatterboxpro
https://www.linkedin.com/in/marjoryleposky/
https://www.instagram.com/meleposky/

J. M. SILVERLEAF

Jillian Silverleaf is an author with a learning disability and is passionate about people with disabilities of all ranges and ages learning to read. She taught special education with an emphasis on autism and down syndrome, ranging in age from pre-k to adult.

After retiring from teaching, Jillian went back to school and received a Master's degree in acupuncture.

Jillian currently lives in Virginia, USA, with her best friend and partner, LK and their three fur babies: two rescued chihuahuas, Rose and Lily, and a very formal cat who wears a permanent tuxedo.

Pamela K. Kinney

Pamela K. Kinney gave up long ago trying not to listen to the voices in her head and has written award-winning, bestselling horror, fantasy, science fiction, and poetry, along with nonfiction ghost books ever since. Her poem "Dementia" won "Best Poem" in the Critters Readers Poll 2020. She also had a horror short story, "Family Inheritance," and a poem, "Ghosts," included in the Journal of the Virginia Writers Club, Spring 2021, and a horror short story, "Death of the Apostrophe," in the spring issue of Siren Call Publications.

Pamela and her husband live with one crazy black cat (who thinks she should take precedence over her mistress's writing most days). Pamela has also acted on stage and film and investigates the paranormal for episodes of Paranormal World Seekers for AVA Productions. She is a member of Horror Writers Association and Virginia Writers Club. You can learn more about Pamela K. Kinney at http://www.PamelaKKinney.com.

JENNIFER KYRNIN

Jennifer Kyrnin is a professional web designer and web developer with over 25 years of experience in the field. She has written seven books on web design and HTML, as well as writing and starring in several video courses for Pearson Education. Her short fiction has appeared in Meniscus Journal and she is currently working on a novel about computer-literate dryads. Jennifer lives on a small farm outside Seattle with her family and lots of animals.

S. P. MOUNT

Stephan considers himself 'against the grain'–a disposition that bemuses lifelong friends. Prolific, his works include literary and speculative fiction; he often delves into a uniquely nonsensical part of his  psyche simply for self-amusement, hoping others will find it funny, too. Darker aspects of his writing often arise to surprise, and even shock even him, but generally he roots for the underdog, has a penchant for writing likeable bad guys, and voices a strong aversion to clichés, such as apple pie that tastes 'just like granny used to make'.

From Scotland, Stephan studied the art of writing at college in Vancouver where he now owns a small business with his rescue dog, Quentin, who when all is said and done, is the senior partner of the operation. His work is published in various anthologies, as well literary journals–some of which may be found here: https://amzn.to/36Vf63m.

MICHAEL GORE

Michael, known to his fans as AuthorMike, is the author of 12 books, including a number 1 bestseller. He has done book signings and lectures in numerous countries and dozens of states, sold movie/television rights, been in documentary films and had his books featured in hundreds of media outlets around the world.

Mike's writing ranges from biographies for film legends like, Kane Hodder and Tom Savini, to novels and short story collections. His novel, *Pieces*, with co-author Rebecca Rowland was billed as an "Essential Read" by *Rue Morgue* Magazine. Currently he is writing a paranormal-themed book for Simon and Schuster.

Under his pen name, Michael Gore, he has published numerous short stories and released the hit short story collections, *Tales from a Mortician* and *Skeletons in the Attic*. The stories from those books are currently being optioned for a movie. A third collection as Gore will be released in the fall of 2022 with a fourth, a Halloween themed collection set to be released in the fall of 2023.

GREG PATRICK

A dual citizen of Ireland and the states, Greg Patrick is an Irish/Armenian traveler poet and the son of a Navy man. Also, a son of the Traveling  People, he is a former Humanitarian aid worker who worked with great horses for years. He loves the wilds of Connemara and Galway in the rain where he has written many stories. Greg spent his youth in the South Pacific and Europe. He currently resides in Galway, Krakow, and sometimes the states. He now writes and travels. His writing has appeared in several international publications including Celtic Nations Magazine, Lothlorien Press, Irish Arts and Entertainment, and Cannery Row Press.

Blame it on the Pumpkin

E. W. FARNSWORTH

BRIT AUSTIN ILLUSTRATION

Brit Austin (*they/she*) is an illustrator & artist whose work conjures the whimsical macabre and dark folklore. Their art is inspired by fairytales, the

occult, and the Death Positive movement. Their work combines mixed media with a dash of wit and magic to create vibrant book and narrative gallery work.

When they are not drawing, you can find them reading a library book with their favorite cuppa, wandering nature, or curiously exploring the whimsy of the dark & fantastical. They are currently living in Richmond, VA with their demonic cat.

Find them at www.britaustin.com.

PORTFOLI-MO

Portfoli.Mo (they/them) is a graphic designer and artist. They sell their art and designs as prints, charms, lanyards, stickers, button badges, enamel pins, and totes. They also write stories, design book wraps, and take on short contract work that uses their skills.

While their method and medium change, you can usually identify Mo's style by its rounded lines, rainbow colors, and sparkles.

DreamPunk Press
Dreamer-in-Chief

Tara Moeller (she/they) is Dreamer-in-Chief at DreamPunk Press, which means she's the editor-in-chief and primary bottle-washer for every project.

She is also an author of adult fiction in several genres and tries to blog at www.taramoeller.com; of course all her books are available from www.dreampunkpress.com. If you check her out on Amazon, there are a couple of other anthologies she has stories in.

Tara also writes speculative YA fiction as E. G. Gaddess and has won awards for her contemporary YA as Zahra Jons.

Blame it on the Pumpkin